A CHOICE FORGED BY FATE

TANYA DECLERCQ

A Choice Forged By Fate

www.GeminiAuthor.com

A Choice Forged By Fate

To follow/support the author, please check out her webpage at:
www.GeminiAuthor.com

There you will find a blog, newsletter for updates and exclusive opportunities, a chat option, contact form, links to all her social media accounts, as well as her published work.

Editor: Kristina Parker

Formatting: Black Bow Publishing

Cover Art: Gemini Moon Publishing, LLC with Christopher DeClercq

ISBN (Hardcover): Coming Soon
ISBN (Paperback): 979-8-9897401-1-6

CHAPTER 1
~ JENNA ~

"Eve?" I asked louder than intended.

We stood in the office; the demon stood in the corner, studying us, while the Fate sat in the chair closest to the desk. She appeared in awe of everything around her. From the little I knew; I suppose that was to be expected. She had spent her life with her sisters, never leaving their home.

"Calm yourself, Jenna. We don't know if this is true." Carissa spoke up, but I could hear the tremor in her words.

Stalking toward Vanessa, it took every ounce of restraint I had to not grip her delicate neck and throw her against the wall. I wanted to take my anger out on someone, and Vanessa made a glowing target, her golden eyes staring up at me. Red hair hung all the way down her back. Skin, unblemished, begged to have hands roam over soft flesh. Eyes that shone with innocence could not hide the knowledge swirling within. How could someone who sees the fates of all be so naïve and so aware at the same time?

Years had to pass for me to become comfortable being a vampire. Marcus had taken me on a whirlwind of experiences, spanning centuries, until we finally parted ways. Taking up with The Agora, I was really living life on my own terms, however brief. I lost all that with the interruption provided by Death and this Fate.

"Eve." Her soft voice rang out.

"Don't call me that." I ground out.

"You must recall who you are. If you do not..." Vanessa's words trailed off as a shimmer flashed across her eyes.

"I know who I am. Fuck! Every time I get comfortable with who I am, someone comes to screw it all up. I am so over this shit. Victor. Marcus. That jackass Death, and now... now this fucking Fate wants to tell me I am some reincarnation of some twisted bible story."

"For hell's sake, you bitch a lot." Ademia chimed in, while casually cleaning her nails with a curved dagger normally kept at her hip.

"Fuck off, demon."

"Can't. Still have the terms of your victory to settle." She groaned and slid from the arm of the chair she had perched upon, landing in the seat.

"Enough!" Joanna shouted, "Ademia, go to your suite and we will discuss everything later. Carissa, if you are going to take over, then you need to speak up in these matters."

Carissa shrunk slightly where she sat behind the desk, as if she were a toddler put in time out. I felt my eyes swirl from red to black to white, then back again. The whirlpool of emotions refused to let any single essence dominate for more than a moment. I needed to calm myself but found the task nearly impossible.

"Tell me what you know." My eyes cut to Vanessa. The demon lingered by the door in anticipation.

"Leave." Joanna ordered as an invisible force shoved Ademia through the doorway. The door slammed shut, and the lock clicked with a resounding finality.

Vanessa sat at ease throughout, which only increased my frustration. As my eyes morphed, there was no judgment or hint at what kind of life the Fate led. She was unreadable. Had she done more harm than good in her life? How long did a Fate even live?

"Eve...Jenna must accept who she is, and she must remember her past. The memories are locked away within her. If she does not, then most likely she will lose. This time forever."

"So, what? I have to remember every reincarnation? Relive past lives?" I moved to the bar, filling a glass with bourbon, and bringing it to my lips. I relished the familiar taste as it passed my tongue.

"Life. You have only ever been Eve. You were lost, your energy locked away by someone. Even then, there are things that were done, said, or thought. I can help you start the right path, guide you where you need to go to get back your memories. That is all I can do."

"Can? Or do you mean will?" I turned to look at her.

"Both actually." Vanessa replied plainly.

I damn near growled deep in my chest at her words. As if I didn't have enough to deal with, I get to add little miss cryptic. What was with everyone in my life?

"We will see, Vanessa. Spill it. Keep in mind that I'm dangerously close to not caring if you are the last Fate."

"First, I will stay with Ademia. You will task her with keeping me safe and here on this plane of existence. While she and I remain, Carissa and you will go with Alex and Azrael to Hell. Tell him of your victory and how Ademia is forfeited to you. You can go alone if you feel comfortable for that part. Out of amusement, he will not retaliate anytime soon." The Fate continued as if I hadn't just threatened to fucking kill her.

"That all?" I scoffed.

"No. Then you must find a very special book. One held deep within the Caverns of Time. For that task, the others will have to go with you. The four of you must make the journey together or you will fail."

"Caverns of Time?" Carissa gasped.

"I read about those. No one has ever come out." I glanced at Carissa.

"Then how did they get their name and how does anyone know of the book?" Vanessa asked with sincerity in her voice.

I ground my teeth. Every word that flitted free from her lips landed like a brick in my chest. The truth of what she said coursed through my veins, urging my feet to move. An excitement grew from within that this was the last piece of the puzzle. But was it?

"Fine. Find those brothers. We leave in an hour. I will go to Hell on my own."

"The fun never stops." I grumbled to myself.

I knew I could walk through any of the doors I passed to reach my destination, yet I delayed. Hell wasn't exactly high on my list of favorite places to visit; I had only been twice. Both times were in service to The Agora. Neither time did I have the displeasure of meeting the Devil himself. I suppose there really is a first time for everything when you are practically immortal.

With a deep sigh, my steps ceased in front of a set of double doors. If I were to stay here, these doors would take me into the garden. A place I had been so fond of before, not knowing that the fountain was somehow tied to me. The newfound knowledge made the choice between the garden and Hell seem like choosing between the lesser of two evils. Narrowing my gaze, they opened on their own as I began to move.

Hell wasn't entirely what most expected. Though part of what you got depended on who you were. For me, the place resembled a field of flowering bushes that sprayed a mist into the air. Black barbs covered bright green vines, which moved to slice the flesh of those who were unfortunate enough to walk too close. The grass appeared lush; appearances were deceiving. The ground was as rough as broken glass on the pads of any bare feet. In the distance, fires raged across the horizon. The typical version of Hell most stories depicted, complete with rivers of blood that were aflame and a river of souls cutting the landscape in half, which gave the scene an eerie melody of mourning.

What I did find off-putting about the visits here were the tiles that rose wherever I went. My feet never touched the ground. The vines recoiled as if they feared the stone that disappeared as soon as my foot left it. For some reason, this strange protection always set my nerves on edge. Now, I wondered if this happened because I was Death, or half Death. Death was something no one could avoid forever. A force of nature that was the gateway to this eternity.

The path took me deeper into Hell than I had traveled previously. Beyond the field were derelict buildings somehow hidden until I neared. Some had toppled over, while others stood tall against the reddish sky. Another trick of Hell, how the landscape changed in an instant without warning. On the air was the scent of decay mixed with blood, sweat, and a sickly-sweet aroma I couldn't quite identify. I wasn't certain where I was going, but I continued on regardless.

Feeling like hours had passed, I cursed under my breath. How was I supposed to get Lucifer to speak to me? Screw him if he didn't want to talk. I needed to get on with it and had the others waiting for me. I turned around when the landscape again morphed into a wasteland devastated by volcanoes. The ground was sharp rock, with bubbling pits of lava scattered about. Heat washed over me in a flash, causing my skin to bead with sweat.

"Fuck this." I mumbled.

Through the abandoned buildings where screams began to rise up, I walked. The scent of blood became thick in the air. Demons were at play. There was no mistaking their handiwork when I saw body parts begin to appear on the vines. They sawed the limbs and organs, grinding them up until they dripped down to the soil beneath. The flowers in the bushes changed from a bright pink color to a deep red. I paused in awe of what was transpiring. Never had I spent enough time here to bear witness to even a fraction this world offered.

The intestines wrapped around the vine reminded me of a sausage casing being filled in reverse. Hearts, lungs, livers, arms, legs, genitalia from both sides appeared within the mayhem. A dripping sound brought my eyes upward to take note of the heads resting on pikes, alive, trying to scream as their eyes filled with horror. Instinct told me they could feel what was happening to their bodies below.

"Does this entice you?" A voice sounded around me.

"No." I spat out.

"Pity." One short word spoken as the world around disappeared like a curtain falling to reveal what really waited.

"A pleasure to have you here." Lucifer's voice was masculine, yet somehow not what I expected. His voice was not as deep as Death's or Marcus'.

I shook my head, an internal scolding to be thinking of them now. Gone were the tiles beneath my feet. Here were pristine white walls with light brown accents. A large rug covered the white marble floor leading up to where he sat on a very large wooden throne. Everything was bright, clean, and here the only aroma was that of jasmine.

"I have come to tell you that I bested your demon, Ademia. Her life was forfeited to me." I stood my ground in preparation for a battle that did not come.

"I see."

He vanished, only to reappear behind a bar that had not existed before. Pouring a glass full of a strange, iridescent, green fluid, he smirked. Another blink of my eyes found him standing behind me, I assumed a silent challenge, so I refused to glance back.

"This is very intriguing, dear Jenna. Very intriguing indeed. Especially since you have no idea why."

That had me spinning on my heels to face nothing...he was no longer there, despite the fact that I could still feel the warmth from his breath on my cheek. Looking back, he rested at the front of the room once more. Lazily, he crossed his legs while sipping from his glass.

"What is to stop me from keeping you here with me? You are in my domain. Have taken possession of my property."

"I did so under the laws upheld by The Agora. Your demon accepted the challenge, and she lost. Accept it or try to keep me here and lose more of your pets. Either way, I have done what I came here for and will be on my way."

"So headstrong. You can leave for now, my dear. Rest assured we will meet again."

"Story of my fucking life, Lucifer." I mumbled.

He grinned widely, revealing a mouth full of sharp teeth. A curt nod was the only real reply to my statement.

The world shifted around me, tilting in every direction, forcing me to close my eyes. I kept them closed until I felt a strong hand grasp my shoulder and opened them to find Alexander staring at me.

CHAPTER 3
~ CARISSA ~

Jenna left the room without another word. Mother left right after with only a quick word over her shoulder indicating that she would get the McKenzie brothers and meet me in the garden in an hour.

Arriving before everyone else, I had been sitting there staring at the fountain. How many times had I run through here as a little girl? Better yet, how many times had I told my mother it wasn't fair that Eve had been killed by those in her own village because of the jealousy of another? Now I sit here waiting for her, or a part of her. Somehow, the story seemed to be lacking something that escaped me. A blur hid away a truth from sight but caused a knotted feeling deep in my gut.

"Tsk, tsk, Beauty. Frowning like that will leave lines on that otherwise perfect face." A voice sounded from my left, deep with a gravely tone hinting at the raw, unhinged nature of the man.

"Azrael." Forcing his name from my lips left a bittersweet taste.

"Come now, Beauty. My judgement was passed, my servitude to The Agora for the next hundred years assured, and my promise to satisfy any need you have."

"The last part you added, but I don't need anything from you other than to aid others." Even as I said the words, I wondered if things would be different if he hadn't killed so many innocents. The act was unforgivable even to save the Fates. Especially when they still died in the end. I suppose that was partly because we stopped the last ritual. He couldn't have done it forever anyway.

He sat beside me, his thigh lightly touching mine. Heat rose up from my chest to the tips of my ears, causing me to shift further away from him. Azrael had always had the same effect on me, whether I wanted to admit it or not. No mirror was needed to know my skin was glowing with a soft pink hue from the thoughts he conjured.

Azrael looked exactly like his brother Alexander, with one exception. In Azrael's left eye, there was a small black mark resembling a crescent moon. Also, if he felt any emotion, he never showed it, his eyes remained a brilliant white. Alexander's eyes at least gave you an indication of his mood or feelings if you were close enough to see. They ranged from clear white around his pupil to an off white that reflected hints of a soft yellow or blue.

"You ready?" Jenna's voice tore me from the path my mind seemed determined to travel.

"Yes." I stood to join her and Alexander, who had come in just behind her.

Azrael wasted no time falling in step at my side, standing so close his arm brushed against mine. I hid the internal groan while ignoring the shiver rushing over my body. Alexander cut his eyes from mine to his brother's with a look I had never seen before.

Leading them all to the back corner, I closed my eyes, feeling the ivy in front of us slowly spreading to reveal the hidden door. This was a special passage leading to an area no true *door* could ever reach, including the others in The Agora. The Caverns of Time were not a place many ventured. Treasure hunters or those arrogantly wishing to make a name for themselves were the only ones who had even made an attempt in the last hundred years. None of them were seen again.

Admittedly, I wondered about the caverns. Why were they called the Caverns of Time? If no one ever made it out, how *does* anyone know the type of danger that waited within to name it as such?

"Let me go first." Alexander placed himself between the rest of us and the door.

"Ever the knight in shining armor, brother." Azrael mocked as he pushed him aside.

"None of you can enter without me, so I will go first. Jenna, place your hand on my shoulder. You two do the same, with one of you placing your hand on her shoulder." My eyes cut into each brother pointedly.

I watched them all grumble, Alexander insisting on being third in line. If I didn't know better, I would think they were unaware of our destination. After a few deep breaths to clear my head, I held the knob, which began to glow, before opening the door with a silent prayer to the Gods.

I had only ever been here once before. That trip was only to teach me how to travel to this place in case it was ever necessary. As then, I was amazed at the crisp air, the vast formations of rock that surrounded us, and the tingling sensation that permeated my body down to my core.

Apparently, I wasn't the only one that felt it. Studying the rest of our group, each one looked around as if they were searching for something while either flexing their hands or rubbing at their chest. Four powerful beings standing in place trying to assess their surroundings or all delaying entry. For the other three, I wasn't sure. In my case, I struggled internally. While I wanted to get on with this task, I knew one misstep meant we would be lost. The opening to the caverns gaped open ahead of us.

"Who's up for some fun?" Azrael began walking toward the opening, backwards. He gave me a wink, then turned to face the caverns.

He didn't pause as he crossed the threshold. Alexander jogged to catch up, his concern for his brother evident despite their friction. I was thankful that he and Jenna had come to terms with everything that had happened. One day, mother might actually tell me how that meeting went. Azrael's trial had taken my focus at the time.

Jenna and I shared a glance. We stepped in unison towards the men that waited impatiently. We had only made it ten feet into the cavern when the first divide halted our progress. The brothers looked at us with raised brows.

"Do either of you have any idea which way we need to go?" Alexander queried, his look reminding me of a principal I had when mother insisted I attend a mortal school for a year.

"How the fuck would we know?" Jenna bit back.

"Someone is on edge." Azrael quipped.

"Will you all calm down? None of us have been here and there isn't exactly a map available." I hoped to squelch the animosity before it became an issue.

"How the heck did I get mixed up in this?" I whispered to myself.

My eyes took in the cavern. Strange lanterns lined the walls. Rock crept up to meet a ceiling decorated with a few stalactites. The ground was a mixture of dirt and stone that echoed with our steps. The place reminded me of a tomb. A tomb I wanted to leave as soon as possible.

"Jenna, this was a task the Fate said you needed to undertake. You know the way we have to go. Trust your instincts." I nudged her elbow, praying to the Gods I was right.

She sighed, moving to stand between the paths. The three of us remained several feet behind, waiting in anticipation. Why we were here was yet to be determined. Situated between the brothers, my nerves were on edge, causing me to take a single step forward.

"Come on, Jenna. You can do this." I called out to her.

CHAPTER 4
~ JENNA ~

They were all waiting on me. Hell, *I* was waiting on me. I looked between the two openings with uncertainty. There was no pull to either side. Closing my eyes, my focus went to quieting my mind.

"I am a vampire. I am Death. I am a vampire. I am Death." The chant falling from my lips as a plea for some part of me to find the way.

When nothing happened, I sighed. Several minutes passed, causing my aggravation to rise. With more determination, my chant returned. I wasn't sure why, but I knew this would connect me to that invisible compass we were all counting on.

"I am a vampire. I am Death. I am a vampire. I am Death. I am a vampire. I am Death... Fuck it. I am Eve." Upon the last proclamation, I felt it.

Looking to the right, my feet carried me forward. My ears picked up the sound of the others following behind, but I couldn't bring myself to stop or care. Left. Right. Center. Center. Right. Time was lost on me. Sweat dripped down my neck to soak the top of my shirt. My pace didn't slow until I heard my name called out with urgency. My feet halted immediately.

"Jenna. Stop." Alexander commanded.

Glaring over my shoulder, my anger evaporated when I took in the beet red faces behind me. They were all panting. Carissa appeared on the verge of hyperventilating. Alexander watched her with concern in his eyes. Azrael attempted to rub her back, only to have her jerk away. She leaned against the wall, her legs shaking. I walked back to her, nodding toward a rock nearby where she could sit.

Alexander narrowed his gaze at me. I could feel the irritation rolling off him. Part of me wondered if it was for himself or for her. She seemed oblivious, but I saw how both men watched her a little too closely. Alexander was always the picture of a gentleman, whereas Azrael was still on my list of men I would like to kill. Slowly. With a spoon.

"We have been walking for hours." Carissa broke the silence, but it was her words that stunned me. I hadn't realized we had walked for that long.

"Let's eat and rest for a moment." I went into the bag Carissa had set on the ground, knowing she was always prepared.

We sat without a word, drinking water and enjoying the sandwiches, which I didn't realize I needed so badly. They didn't fully satisfy my appetite, though they would do for now. As if reading my thoughts, Carissa cleared her throat.

"Do you need to feed?"

"Thought I just did." I smirked.

"Seriously." Azrael blurted out.

"What is your problem now?" Alexander intervened.

"She is not feeding off her. She should have fed before we came here if she needed to. We are not her walking buffet."

I grabbed Azrael by the throat, lifting him until his feet lost their claim on the ground. My eyes swirled from red to black. Part of me wanted to laugh. If it were not for me standing on a slightly elevated piece of stone, I would not have been tall enough to make my point.

"I think I am just fine." I ground out while allowing my eyes to morph to a bright white that made him close his own.

"Enough. Damn it, Jenna. I swear if you had a dick, I would tell you all to put them away."

"You must be pissed. You actually swore, Carissa." I laughed, allowing Azrael to drop back down.

"No one would ever truly believe you are hundreds of years older than I am." Carissa fought to keep the smile from her lips. A battle she quickly lost when I gave her a wink.

"Ok. We need to keep going. The longer we delay, the more likely we are to get lost in here." Alexander scolded.

I made my way back toward the openings. Eyes closing to connect with that invisible thread that pulled me through, I opened them again when there was nothing. *Shit. Shit. Shit.* I tried again...and again...and again. Stopping seemed to have cut the connection.

"What's wrong?" Alexander approached.

"I can't feel it anymore. Fuck!" I shouted in frustration.

"I can." Azrael spoke more to himself than to us.

CHAPTER 5
~ AZRAEL ~

There was a strange push and pull pulsating through my entire body. I barely registered my feet moving or the voices of those around me. Now I understood why we had to basically scream to get Jenna to stop. The only voice able to cut through the haze was Carissa's. That didn't surprise me in the least. She always had an influence over me whether she realized, or wanted it, or not.

Continuing forward, the twists and turns blurred in front of me until the gray stone faded completely away. In their place were the walls of The Agora. A younger Carissa stood before me in a warm pink dress. The spaghetti straps showed faint tan lines and for the first time I could recall, I yearned to see how far down they went.

Carissa was celebrating her twentieth birthday with her mother. Laughter filled the hallway, ringing out from them both and a man that stood with his hand on her lower back. Without thought, the bones in his index finger snapped. He yelped in pain, Carissa and Joanna jumping into action to tend to his wound.

Two things about the event bothered me. One, why did I react so strongly to seeing her? Two, how could I harm someone within the walls of The Agora? I rushed through the doors to my brother's dwelling before they could see me. I remained with my back against his door, our eyes meeting, and the question forming was one I knew I couldn't answer.

"Do not ask. Believe me, you don't want to know." I told him.

"With you. Probably not. So why don't we just focus on why you're here." Alexander spoke.

"Yes. Why did you summon me, dear brother?" I smiled widely at his annoyance.

"There has been word passed down." Alexander paused.

"This isn't the time for your cryptic bullshit. Get to the point so I can be on my way."

"When did things turn so sour between us?" He asked.

"If that's what you want to discuss, then I am out of here." I turned to go, but his words made me freeze.

"We will be facing a great danger and if we don't face it together, we will die." Alexander, ever the cold bastard, just stared at me, waiting for my reaction.

"Is that all?" Was that an asshole response? Yes. Did I care? Only a little.

I was ostracized by my family years ago because I refused to live by their rules. If ever there was a family that needed to adjust to the times, it was them. So why, as I turned to leave his place, do I feel a pit grow within my stomach? Stupid question. For all their faults, I would die to protect my brother. Even with the stick shoved up his ass.

He called after me, a faint sound that faded into nothing as I closed the door behind me. Even if it hadn't, I doubt I would have heard him. I only saw her. Many believe only shifters or Lycans have destined mates. For almost all, that is true, even among witches and warlocks. There is only one exception. My family. Apparently, they made a deal eons ago that one day a member of our family would join another family to save the world.

That story rang in my ears now. This infatuation had me wanting to leave here and never return again. That damn mark in my eye, the alleged declaration that I was the one betrothed to some unknown woman. Now, I felt truth in that, and I was certain who the woman was meant to be. She deserved better. I would never be worthy of her on my best day. Walking up to her, I felt compelled to speak to her one last time.

"Carissa."

She turned with a slight smile. Her distress was evident over the injury to her *friend*.

"Azrael. Hello, I'm sorry. Things are a little busy at the moment."

"I know. I just wanted to wish you a happy birthday." Leaning in, my lips found her cheek, and the contact rippled through every nerve in my body.

It was obvious she felt it too. She pulled back, her fingers pressing where my lips had been.

"Uh, thank you." Her voice trailed off.

"You're welcome, Beauty."

CHAPTER 6
~ CARISSA ~

Something was very wrong. The air held a charge that made my hair stand on end. More than that, Azrael had fallen silent. Alexander tried to speak to him, but he just kept walking as if we no longer existed. My fear increased the further we traveled. Alexander seemed to share my feelings while Jenna walked on as if we were on a lovely midday stroll.

"We have to do something." I could no longer keep quiet.

"What exactly would you like us to do? We knew we would likely encounter something strange. He's not hurt. We're not hurt. Till one or both of those things change, I say we continue on." Jenna replied.

I knew Jenna was right but that didn't mean I liked it. Playing along, we walked deeper into the caverns. The air grew thicker, the temperature dropping with every passing minute. Those weren't the only differences. The passage was narrowing. So focused on our surroundings, my brain took a few seconds to register the words I heard escape Azrael.

Those words were the last he had said to me before disappearing for a few years. Not so much disappearing if I were being honest but avoiding The Agora and me. Yet every time our paths had crossed, he kept that same nickname for me. He hadn't said my name, to me at least since that day. I realized that in some way, I missed it.

"He's lost in the past." I muttered when realization sank in.

"I know." Jenna stated plainly.

"We have to help him." Alexander added with a slightly panicked tone.

It was then that I noticed Azrael flicker. He literally flickered like the strange torches that lined every wall to light our way. This is what happens. A memory consumes those that enter. They are lost to it, fading into that single moment. A question popped into my mind, if he was caught in the past, was he even leading us the right way?

He shoved Alexander aside as if he were a web that floated in his path when his brother attempted to stop him. Jenna walked a little way behind, one glance in her direction confirmed that her mind was playing out one scenario after another on what to do. I, however, couldn't stand idly by doing nothing.

Running up to him, I walked backwards calling his name. Frustrated, I halted causing our chests to collide. Briefly his eyes focused then he was lost once more. I raised my hand to his cheek, fear making my eyes water.

"Azrael. Azrael, please wake up. Come back to us. We need you. Azrael?!" He stopped when my voice raised in an exasperated plea, his face contorted in confusion.

"Beauty?" The word sounded strained to my ears.

"Azrael, darn it! Wake up!" I yelled louder and watched as he flickered one last time, felt him become less real, then was back with us, solid as ever.

"Wh...what happened?" Azrael shut his eyes tight, rubbing them as if he could clear away whatever he was experiencing.

"You were almost lost to a memory." Alexander replied.

Azrael looked down at me, I felt my chest tighten as I took in his gaze and that crescent shaped mark. He was always someone that made me feel both at war and at peace. If that made any sense. This moment was no different.

"We have to continue on." Jenna walked past us.

"I'm fine, leech. Thanks for the concern." Azrael bit back.

"Do you still feel the connection?" I stepped away but kept my eyes on him.

"No. Does anyone else? I think we'll each have our own test that we'll have to pass if we're going to succeed."

What Azrael said seemed to confirm what we each thought as I saw the others nod in agreement. I turned to look at the trail to see if I sensed anything pulling me forward but there was nothing. The only thing I was certain of was that there was more to these memories than being lost. One I worried about voicing.

CHAPTER 7
~ ALEXANDER ~

The second my brother woke, I felt it clamp down. Like a lock slipping into place, I was connected to this place and whatever journey we were all tasked with. This didn't sit well with me, but I couldn't refuse when they came to me saying they needed both of us to accompany Jenna and Carissa. Especially when I learned that the task was to traverse these caverns. Plus, Azrael had immediately agreed when the request was made.

My brother never volunteered for anything, nor did he willingly assist with jobs over the last several years. What had changed, I still didn't know. I asked him many times but got the brush off response with every inquiry. Had I given up? Not entirely. Pressure would get me nowhere though, so I chose my moments to pry without success.

"Why did you come?" I whispered to him now.

"I had to." He stated.

"Why? You answered the summons from Joanna and agreed without hesitation."

"I couldn't let her..." his voice trailed off. Clearing his throat, he continued, "This was too important."

"This? Or her?" I queried but only received a glaring look.

When he stepped away, I studied our surroundings. Here the cave started off wide, with a soft dirt floor and dry, stone walls reaching up into a perfectly arched ceiling. I noted that the walls were starting to show signs of moisture. On the air, I faintly detected the scent of moss. It reminded me of the times I scavenged for ingredients in the forbidden woods.

I took a step forward, not really thinking. If only I could be back in that forest instead of some cave, I wasn't sure I'd ever leave. The journey had been extremely important to me yet one I had not thought of since. A witch within the northwest coven foretold of a glowing silver berry that would allow a person to change their destiny. A way to change fate was rare indeed.

A couple more minutes passed when I blinked to see that forest. No longer did hard stone fill my gaze. Replaced with the lush soft floor of green grass, wildflowers, and leaves that had already started to fall. Sunlight pierced the high canopy, where it could, to reflect off the dew refusing to dissipate. Little sparkles of light danced as I walked further into the woods.

"Where was I just going?" I whispered as confusion settled over me.

"Berries. Yes, I need to find the berries. I will set things right this time." Excitement hastened my steps until I was almost running.

I failed last time. Let the fear in me stop me from doing what I knew was right. What didn't make sense to me was why? My memory around the decision was blurred. There was the berry, shining brightly in a small clearing, my fingers pressed gently into the flesh with my request, then I am turning around. Walking back out of the woods without having eaten the berry, having no recollection as to why I changed my mind consumed me for months. Potions, talismans, research...nothing told of that being part of the issue with the fruit. Ultimately, I concluded I had been a coward. Another act that had driven a wedge between my brother and me.

Any chance at improving one's situation always came with risks, the balance had to be maintained. That was something that could not be changed and the only thing that kept many from being too greedy. The more one attempted to tip the scales in their favor, the harder the consequences hit to balance back out. A lesson our parents had learned which led to their agreement in the prophecy.

The prophecy. My sole reason for coming to these woods. I knew my brother hated being told what to do. Azrael living his whole life with the knowledge his destiny was sealed to another, had never sat well with him. He wanted a choice. Freedom. Hell, I couldn't blame him. That he didn't and I did was one reason there was an underlying animosity between us. He didn't blame me, but he felt life was unfair. The chip on his shoulder growing each year as a result.

We may be as different as night and day, but he was still my brother and I wanted to help. With the berry, I could wish for him to have a choice, so he didn't have to shoulder the responsibility. Then, as now, I tried to think of the right words. Another trick to any magic, wording. The children's stories about being careful what you wish for were true. I also had to make sure I didn't make matters worse.

My request is to ease the burden placed on my brother. May the Fates see fit to allow choice in the prophecy that will bring him peace. To make life fair where the scales were tipped.

I nodded feeling satisfied with my request. My journey reaching its end shortly after. There it was as before. Sunshine filtered through the canopy in a stream that highlighted the bright silver berries. My pace slowed, anticipation mixing with a pit of dread. Reaching the bush, I ran my hand over the soft leaves in a silent request for permission.

"If you proceed, much more will change than you realize. For more people than you intend." An older voice cracked; a figure no taller than the bush stepping out from behind.

"What do you mean?"

They stood there reminding me of some rounded version of Yoda with wrinkled brown skin, yellow eyes, and small hands ending in long claw-like nails. Looking down, those eyes only locked on mine through the hooded cloak it wore, thin lips curling to reveal sharp teeth.

"You will see. Or you won't. Choice is yours." The thing cackled a sound that made me feel like the temperature dropped to freezing.

"You're the reason I don't remember my decision, aren't you?"

The only response I received was another vile smile. That was all I needed. This conversation was new but felt familiar. Whatever transpired had changed my mind about taking the berry. Part of my mind fought to remind me I was not here, instead I was walking in a cave with others. However, there was a whisper telling me this was a second chance. The hope of not failing my brother a second time, of earning redemption.

Curiosity grew as to what this decrepit creature could possibly have said to make me abandon my brother. Granted he never knew I had come here. Even though this was for him, he would have tried to stop me. Wanting change and being willing to let another sacrifice for that were two entirely different things.

Maybe that's what this place is. A chance to see what could

have been if we made different choices. If things were better, I could see people never wanting to pull themselves out from this dream state. I'd heard enough. That thing talked me out of it before, but not again. What would have happened if I had done it?

"Let's find out." I muttered as I quickly plucked the berry from the bush with my plea in my thoughts.

Popping it into my mouth, I tasted blood, metallic and nauseating that mellowed into a rich dark chocolate. As the taste morphed, a tingling sensation took root from my core throughout my body. I felt hot and cold, my movements sluggish as the air around me grew heavier.

"What's happening?" I asked, not really expecting a response.

"You chose differently this time. Now you tipped the scales or balanced them. Time will tell." The thing croaked.

"Fucking Yoda." I ground out but it was gone and with it the forest.

Back in the cave, Azrael slapped me for what I realized must have been the third or fourth time by the sting of my cheek.

"Yoda? I get blasted to the past and you're fucking around in a Star Wars dream. Guess I know now why I don't see you in any real relationships."

"Fuck off." I shook my head, pain lancing through my skull.

Not able to take a step, the ground became my seat. The others sitting beside me looking exhausted. Even my brother had sweat dripping down his face. Each drinking from their water bottles, no one spoke for several minutes.

"How long was I walking?"

"Hours. We couldn't get you to stop or even slow down. It was like you were on a mission. What did you see in there?" Azrael replied.

"Star Wars." I quipped back not wanting to tell him the truth.

What would it matter though? Not like he could say anything about my own memories. Still, it would mean I would have to admit that I was a coward and had left him to his fate. That was something I couldn't face, not now and likely not ever.

This place seeped into my cells the longer we remained. Why did we have to end up here of all places? I could only hope this book was worth it. One thing was certain, we had almost lost both Azrael and Alexander during their time in, well, time. This was insane but not surprising. Nothing really surprised me anymore.

As a little girl, my mother began training me. What we were and were not allowed to say to others. What we were and were not allowed to do in front of others. The first eight years of my life I believed so many things. Many of which I discovered later were lies. All perpetuated to protect the truth that would put too many in danger. My quiet defiant nature wondered if that was really a fact or another lie.

In this place, one fact I knew but refused to voice. We were seeing moments this place knew we would want to stay in, or we chose somehow. If I told the others this, they would ask how I knew. All I could say was that I did. It didn't help us, so I said nothing. I feared what memory I would be pulled into. Would I be strong enough to leave?

Thinking back on simpler times filled with innocence, I began to walk. Completely aware of my movement yet unable to care. The others could be heard falling in line behind me. Their steps echoed my own. Part of me wanted to glance back at them, make sure they were there and ok. But I didn't. Couldn't. Wouldn't. Somehow it was all the same at the moment.

My mind fluttered to a birthday years ago where I saw Azrael off in the distance only to be distracted by the sudden scream of my then boyfriend. That relationship, like almost all I had since, did not last long. They didn't feel right. Not that they just felt a little off, they felt wrong. The more time passed, the more I would begin to feel sick.

With that thought, I was a baby. My hand raised in front of me was so small, so weak. Mother held me to her chest, her soft voice singing a lullaby I didn't recognize. I strained to listen, to hear what she sang. The words felt important. Minutes passed, each second making me wonder if my infant ears were just making me think there was a mystery where none existed. Trying to figure out why I was brought here to this moment, she surprised me.

"Little one. My sweet Carissa. One day you will understand. It will all become clear. Even among our kind, you are special. A rebirth that rests on your tiny shoulders. You will not carry this burden alone. Our ancestors knew that someone would come along and that another would exist that could join with them to see this through. I never imagined the chosen one would be my own daughter."

I stilled, transfixed by her words but also confused. Was this a confession to one she believed couldn't understand her or did she know I could hear her? Somehow, I understood it to be a mixture of both. Guilt loosened her tongue and hope made her wish that I would somehow remember this one-sided conversation.

Reaching up, I attempted to place my pinky around hers. This was something we did from the time I was a child until this morning. Our secret way of saying I love you and I will always be here for you. Barely able to wrap partially around, I saw a smile spread across her lips. She studied where our fingers touched, an errant tear leaving a trail down her cheek.

"Yes, it will all be ok."

A small laugh escaped that caused her smile to widen. My mother looked so young, so beautiful that my heart swelled. She really has always been so positive. If only she knew I would end up in a cavern reliving a memory I never knew. With a blink, I felt myself falling. My hands gripped something tight, and I felt the wind in my hair change direction as I screamed.

Immediately, someone had their hands over mine. Realization creeping in that within my grasp was a cold chain. My hands were trapped between the hard steel and warm skin. Glancing over my shoulder, I saw a man I didn't know. Before I could ask who he was, he was gone.

I got off the swing, searching for the stranger. No warning bells went off because I was within The Agora grounds. Along the way, realization dawned that I was a teenager now. This was another memory, but this one I vaguely recalled. Stopping mid-step, my path changed from the one taken last time.

"Where did you go?" The question came out quietly.

Walking from the yard to the garden, there was no sign of anyone else around. Defeat began to settle over me when a glimmer caught my eye. Was there someone there or simply a trick of light that led me astray? The only sign I found; I moved closer. The air began to warm, the scent of vanilla mixing in with the jasmine from the flowers all around. That aroma always calmed my nerves though my eyes never stopped searching.

"Hello?" Calling out to the garden felt silly but I couldn't stop myself.

"This and that. That and this. You will never win a kiss."

I spun at the taunting voice that rang out all around me. Young, sweet, yet an undeniable hint of malice. The source eluded me. Taking to moving the blossoms to search the dense foliage, nothing looked amiss. Yet, every few minutes the rhyme repeated.

"Come out here. Now. Make yourself known." Shouting in frustration, I plopped down on a nearby bench.

"Tsk. Tsk. You can try, but all you do is cry. A kiss you want, a kiss you seek but you are just too naïve and weak."

"What is your problem?" It had to be the fairies. They loved mischief. Was I just falling prey to another one of their schemes?

"Wrong you are. Wrong you be. What I am now, you will one day see."

"I hate rhymes." I grumbled.

This was new. When this all actually happened, I had gone through the hallway, bumped into my mother, and ended up in the kitchen eating cookies. Somehow, knowing that only made this feel important.

"Two moons shine bright. One by day. One by night." Laughter erupted so loudly that I covered my ears until silence reigned once more.

Rising, I walked back toward the swings only to collide with a tree. The trunk was sharp, small scrapes rising instantly on my cheek. The entire landscape had changed without my notice. No longer was I safe within The Agora but existed in a forest I had never seen before. A clearing lay straight ahead with a single tree standing tall in the center.

A man stood staring up at the branches, a smile on his face. There was another creeping in the shadows on the other side who commanded my attention. I could feel the rage rolling off him in waves. Anger. Jealousy. Resentment. Murder. He desired bloodshed above all else. Yet, he was mortal where the other most certainly was not. I held my breath uncertain what was about to happen. Only nothing did.

The man in the center strode off toward the south while the other emerged to examine the tree. A sadness consumed me when he snapped one branch off before leaving. I walked to see if there was anything special about the tree but found it to be ordinary. What could make two men obsess so much over one simple tree?

I picked a cherry from the nearest branch and savored the tart taste as the juice coated my tongue. Picking a few more, I shoved them in my pockets then went to see if I could find either of the men. Instead, a few steps from the tree found me barreling into Jenna.

"What the fuck?" She cursed with her hands gripping both my shoulders tight enough that I knew they would be bruised.

"What's wrong?" I asked while shaking the fog from my thoughts.

She sidestepped with her hand gesturing less than a few feet in front of me. There was a great hole in the floor. The torch she grabbed and tossed down never offering a sound if it had ever found the bottom.

"You damn near killed yourself. If I hadn't been bored of you walking so slow, you would have."

"Thank you." I replied unable to keep the quiver of fear that chilled me from my voice.

"That's it. We are heading back." The angered tone of Azrael cut in.

"Like hell we are." Jenna retorted.

As if the cave was alive and listening, a large boulder fell from nowhere to cut off our retreat. Azrael and Alexander leapt into action trying to demolish or move the heavy weight with magic to no avail. We were trapped. The only option remaining was to continue. For the first time, I truly wondered if we would ever leave.

CHAPTER 9
~ JENNA ~

This was insane. How could we think we could come in there and leave with some book when so many failed for eons? Even with the magic the other's possessed and with my *gifts*, we were being outmatched by a fucking piece of carved out earth. I wanted to wring Vanessa's scrawny neck or better yet, tear into it with my fangs and drink every last drop. I wonder if a Fate's blood was different than any others I had savored.

My thirst kicked up a notch as I imagined her blood flowing over my tongue. The crimson flood that waited behind the thin veil. Every time I sank my fangs into someone, there was a euphoric sensation riding the coattails of the nourishing river. It was the cause for lesser vampires' descent into blood lust. What those who had control even called monsters, rippers, and blood junkies. Unlike the mortal's programs, almost none ever recovered from their addiction. Instead, they became mere animals, instinct demanding they feed. It was the only thing their minds seemed to think of.

"Jenna." Carissa's pure voice derailed my thoughts.

I looked her way wondering if I had brought them all to their deaths. Maybe there would be a sacrifice required to get the book. Perhaps even three sacrifices. Time would tell. Of that I was certain.

"We are close. We're very close in fact."

"Great. So, do you feel where we have to go now? I will gladly pass on another trip down memory lane." Alexander stated flatly.

"No. We are on our own now." I informed them.

"Wait, we all get mind fucked and you get to just stroll the fuck on? How the fuck does that make any sense? What is it that makes you so goddamn special?" Azrael cut in, but Alexander placed his hand on his brother's shoulder in an attempt to calm him.

"Don't forget the prophecy around who she is." Alexander whispered.

"Vampire, assholes. I can hear you even when you whisper." I tapped my ear.

"What the hell is this prophecy now?" I crossed my arms waiting.

Azrael pushed past me with a grumble, "Everyone has a damn prophecy. Let's go."

These two were not going to tell me anything, unfortunately. Right now, I didn't have the time to play their little game either. Walking ahead, we all stopped when we came to another junction. In silence we studied both passages. It didn't take a mind reader to know we were all thinking the same thing or rather trying to feel something. Worry was soaking into each of us in its own way.

What's worse is that Azrael's words had been rattling around in my head since we began walking. Why was I led like a puppet while they were all lost in a memory? I had more memories than all of them combined for this place to choose from. Did their memories hold something mine didn't? We never really talked about what everyone saw. Was that a mistake?

Taking a step to the right, an earthquake erupted but the falling debris did little to scare us. Not when from the ground rose sharp stalagmites. Stumbling around while trying to discern where the next spike would rise, I fell back against the wall. In that moment everything stilled.

"Everyone ok?" Carissa called out though both men were already rushing to her side.

"Yes, we're fine. Are you ok?" Alexander examined her for injury even as he asked.

"Thank goodness. What was that?" Carissa exhaled.

"An earthquake, Carissa. You know. Ground shaking. Sometimes splitting open. Though the stabbing rocks were interesting." I joked before coughing hard.

"JENNA!" Carissa screamed as her eyes took in the blood dripping from my mouth.

Slumped against the wall unable to move, they huddled around until a gasp left Carissa's lips. The sadness I saw in her eyes told me things were as bad as I currently felt.

"This is going to hurt." Alexander said as he grabbed hold of my body.

"Just get me off this damn rock, Alexander."

A solemn nod was the only warning I had before he lifted me from my pike and settled me on the ground. The second I was free I felt the blood escaping like a waterfall from the gaping hole in my back that punctured my lung on its way out of my chest. I could, and had, survived almost everything but losing so much blood was not something I had tested.

"You have to feed." Carissa was already moving her hair to the side, leaning closer so her neck was almost at my lips.

"The fuck." Azrael yanked her away before I could bite.

"What are you doing? She has to feed or she is going to die."

"The amount of blood she would need from you will kill you," He cursed under his breath, a hand slipping through the silver white locks of his hair, "Fucking Hell. If she must feed, then she will from us. Enough from both of us should heal her."

Not giving Carissa the opportunity to argue, he shoved his wrist in my face while he looked the other way. Right or wrong, I needed it. The pool growing under my ass was evidence enough of that truth. Not waiting to see if he changed his mind, I bit down perhaps a touch harder than necessary.

I greedily drank of his essence. Taking as much as he dared offer before he yanked his hand away and Alexander's took his place. Whether the extent of my wound or the dampening effects of the cave, their blood was not enough. Each savory taste of their life force confirmed their own strengths and that they were brothers. Both had a flavor reminiscent of licorice, tolerable but not to my preference.

"You're not healed. Why isn't she healing?" Carissa's voice sounded like she was on the verge of hysterics.

I looked over at her realizing just how much of a friend she considered me to be. In that moment, I realized I reciprocated that emotion. Other than Marcus, I hadn't felt close to anyone after losing my parents. Even the women I began helping gain freedom from their oppressing situations had held little true concern for me. More so, it was a victory against any would be tormentors. Triumph over the Victors of the world, no matter their species.

Carissa was leaning closer again, her hand immediately

pushing Azrael away when he made a move toward her. She was strong, more so than I think she realized. Even with that knowledge, there was fear in her eyes. Not for my life but something else that hid just out of sight.

Biting into her neck, the thrum of her pulse sent vibrations through my lips. Steadily her heartbeat, a siren song I had learned long ago to ignore. Seconds felt like minutes, the warmth spreading down my throat to every inch of my body. Life. Her blood tasted like a spring morning, a drop of water after days lost in the desert, the first ripe strawberry of the season, everything good, new, and clean. My control begged to be set aside to savor more but I retracted my fangs with a swipe of my tongue over the wound.

As she pulled back, I took in the paleness of her skin knitting back together. My own body accelerated the same. The instant the hole in my lung sealed shut, instinct demanded I take in a deep breath. The trickle which had remained finally ceased with the last cell restored. Getting up, I pulled at my shirt while turning my head to survey the damage.

"Motherfucker. I liked this shirt and these pants. This is why I can't have nice things." Dusting the dirt off my ass and hands, I studied each of them in turn.

Alexander stood glancing at Azrael and Carissa. Carissa assured him she was ok between gulps of water. Internally I wondered how long it would be till Azrael made a move. Anyone with eyes could see he wanted her. Well, anyone other than Carissa. The woman was a clueless as a virgin in a whorehouse. Taking in Alexander one more time, I smirked, maybe if Azrael didn't get off his ass, his brother would step in.

CHAPTER 10
~ CARISSA ~

Jenna did not look well. She looked better but not herself. My mind replayed the scene, Jenna was literally on her toes thanks to the rock that had skewered her. The solid grey form coated in red streams soaking into the ground. The sound when she was pulled off her perch. A sickening sucking noise ending in a soft pop that made me strangely think of when I was a kid enjoying a popsicle. My stomach turned at the idea as much as the loss of blood.

My eyes seemed determined to continuously glance back at the evidence while the others spoke. I only faintly heard them arguing. Azrael was cursing Jenna for having drank more from me than he felt necessary. She of course was saying something snarky about still being thirsty and if he wanted to volunteer. I knew she didn't need to feed anymore. The hole in her shirt showed how her skin had already mended. From what I knew of her, she might feel like she pulled a muscle for a few minutes till even that faded away.

"This will get us nowhere. Will you all please just stop? I am fine. So is everyone else. Enough of the posturing." I begged.

Not for the first time, I felt like I was a teacher wrangling wily students on a field trip. The constant bickering was exhausting but something told me that most of it was the result of none of them having much control over the situation. This wasn't like going after some enemy. Even our surroundings were against us. Though, perhaps I was projecting my own fears onto the others.

"Give me a minute and we can head on." I swept my gaze to each.

"We need to go back. This is not going to work and someone is going to die." Azrael spoke through clenched teeth.

"Afraid of Death?" Jenna laughed.

"Not of you." Azrael stepped toward her.

"No one is going to die." I reassured them knowing I wasn't certain.

We sat in silence for what felt like a few minutes yet a glance at my watch said it had been half an hour. Time here was still an unknown. Either way, we had to keep going. There really wasn't another option and we all knew it.

Rising to my feet, I walked over to Jenna with a nod. She rose at the same time Azrael and Alexander did. Heading deeper into the cave, I slowly realized that we were on a downward slope. The angle becoming more severe the longer we went till I had to bend my knees to keep from falling forward.

"If this gets any worse, we will have to slide on our asses." Alexander chimed in.

"Who didn't love the slide as a kid?" Azrael snorted.

"They weren't much of a thing when I was a child." Jenna cut back.

Our conversation was interrupted by a sudden drop; we

stood at the precipice. Ten feet away, the path continued. The void between did not offer a hint at what was below. To the right and left were very narrow ledges one might be able to use to get around. A single misstep would mean answering that question of what waited at the bottom.

"Hug the wall and you should be fine." Alexander stated.

I watched him and Azrael split up. Each of them took a side and began to slide as tight to the wall as possible. When they both reached the other side, they motioned for us to go. Staying to the left, Azrael reached out to help me.

"Stop." Jenna said firmly, "That isn't the right way."

"What are you talking about?" I queried, confusion making me halt where I stood halfway along the ledge.

"Something is telling me that we need to go down. Everyone avoids what they fear. The unknown. What they think is certain death. Hell, even a change can send some into a spiral." She wasn't looking at us when she responded, her eyes fixed on the darkness.

"You want to give a speech now?" Alexander almost shouted.

"You're out of your fucking mind. Carissa don't listen to her. Give me your hand and we will get out of this." Azrael stretched further.

"Jenna, what makes you so certain?" I took a step back toward her.

"This is one of the reasons no one ever comes out. They keep going. Keep looking for what they think they need. No one is willing to take the leap. I don't feel the same pull. Hell, maybe I am out of my mind, but I know this is right. I hope you will follow me but if not, I do hope you find your way home."

"JENNA!" I screamed, almost falling in as I watched her disappear.

"Fucking bullshit! She fucking jumped. She's out of her God damn mind." Azrael stood tall, eyes on the hole she had just leapt into.

"Then so am I." I stepped off the ledge.

In the darkness there was no sound. No light pierced through even when I looked up to where I was just standing. Air rushed by, my hair blowing frantically as I fell deeper and deeper. Trying to call out was no use. Here, I had to focus on breathing to remain conscious. Knowledge that I might slam against a narrowing or the ground at any moment had me second guessing my leap of faith. Yet, there was a strange peace in knowing there was nothing I could do but fall. Fear remained by my side, but acceptance held me in its embrace.

"I'm sorry, mom." I whispered.

"For what?" Jenna asked just as she caught me.

"We're alive." I said as I exhaled.

"You were apologizing for living?" She arched her brow at me.

"No. I..." My reply interrupted when torn from her grip.

"Don't you ever fucking do something that fucking stupid again! You follow this bitch down a goddamn fucked up, 'Alice in Wonderland' wannabe rabbit hole. What the hell is wrong with you?" Azrael's grip on my shoulders hurt, his fingers pressing tighter as he yelled in my face.

"Knock it off." Alexander pulled him away.

Azrael was fuming, Alexander taking a step back from me as if I suddenly burst into flames. *What was wrong with them?* I stopped myself before I could get lost in that mess and turned in a circle to take in where we were. The stone was gone. The musty odor had left with it. Beneath our feet was grass, dark green without a single flower or weed to intrude. Walls the color of a beautiful sunset rose to meet at a night sky overhead.

"If I didn't know any better, I would think we were outside." I smiled a little.

"Another trick, I suppose." Jenna muttered.

On one of the walls, there appeared to be a tower of light. Faint but unmistakable. With it being our only beacon, we walked forward to inspect the image. Only our steps failed to bring the image into focus. Remaining at a distance, we halted our steps after an hour proved a lesson in futility.

"This isn't getting us anywhere." Alexander proclaimed.

"Thank you, Captain Obvious." Jenna retorted.

"Please don't start." I sighed.

I was done with the bickering. My expression must have conveyed so if the downturned gazes were any indication. Each of my companions were strong, each stubborn too. Scattering to pace in different directions, I used the moment to reach out with my own gifts. Unleashing the power within was not something done lightly in my family. Now however, seemed to warrant the act. That was until I felt an opposing force shut me down.

"What the Heavens?" I murmured as an image took root.

"What's wrong?" I asked Carissa when she suddenly fell to her knees.

The dynamic duo of dunces were at her side ready to help her up after making sure she wasn't hurt. Even now I couldn't help the thought from popping up to wonder which of them she would end up with. I could see Alexander being the strong, dependable partner for her. Completely respectable and perfectly boring. Azrael though had killed innocents, for a good cause, but he had still shed blood unnecessarily. I wasn't sure if Carissa could really look passed that. I also wouldn't be surprised if he did it again if he felt it was worth it. At least her life with him wouldn't be dull.

"I saw it." Carissa shakily spoke.

"Saw what?" Alexander asked softly.

"Wings. White wings." Carissa replied as her eyes met mine.

"Fucking Hell." I muttered.

Instantly I knew what she meant, what we had to do. The brothers exchanged a look that would have cost them any game they were playing. They were each lost. No surprise really when I had only recently learned of that added gift of my being. I am sure they both assumed mine would be black, if I had any at all since we didn't really discuss that part earlier.

"Hang on to each other." I commanded boldly while the weight grew heavy on my back.

I saw the faint shadow form on the ground, the way both men took in the appearance. Momentarily, none of them moved. I tried to be patient. Seconds ticking away to chip at that resolve until I could no longer stand it.

"Seriously. Move it or I am leaving your asses here." I crossed my arms under my breasts.

"How do we do this?" Carissa asked when she stepped forward.

"I don't think I can carry all of you, but I don't see what choice we have. I will have to try. Alexander, grab on at my back. Carissa, wrap your arms around my neck, legs around my waist. Azrael, you are going to have to try to hold onto my hand."

"So you can drop me when you *slip*?" He arched his brow.

His position was the most unsecure. Admittedly I knew that when thought of how to carry them all. His death would not bother me in the slightest. How many times had he casually played executioner that we didn't know about?

"She won't." Carissa chimed in. Her eyes silently pleading with me not to let him die.

"You have my word. For her sake." I confirmed.

We looked ridiculous. I wasn't even sure I could carry them all. Hell, I hadn't even really flown solo yet. Stretching out my wings, I had to be careful of their movement with Alex at my back and Carissa clinging to me. I wanted a free hand though in case I had to catch her if she slipped. After a few attempts, I felt comfortable enough to rise.

Azrael clasped my wrist as I did his. He was putting his life in my hands or wings. They all were. Leaving the ground, we found that the ceiling that had appeared to be painted had to be magical. Wind began to blow around us. I was flying. Their weight was barely noticeable as I soared higher. The clearing of Carissa's throat bringing me back on task.

Setting my sight on the beacon, I started that way. The light growing brighter as we finally neared.

CHAPTER 12

~ AZRAEL ~

If our magic worked, we would not have needed the escort. Alas, I hung from the fucking leech as she carried us all toward what I hoped was our final test. Too many times I had thought Carissa was going to be hurt or worse. To watch that bitch feed from her almost tore the last of my composure. Only my brother and Carissa stopping me from trying my best to end her.

My heart continued to assault me in time with flashes of Carissa jumping after Jenna. I didn't even hesitate in following her. I didn't like this impulse; this hold she had over me. I resisted it every chance I got. Tell that to my eyes though as they keep looking up to make sure her grip is tight around Jenna's neck. I am not worthy of her. She deserves a good man. I cannot be that, even for her.

With that thought in mind, I force my attention back to our destination just in time to see a balcony. Jenna wasting no time in dropping my ass on the strange foundation, flying up a few feet then landing.

"Testing if it was safe?" I ask not hiding my anger.

"Better you than any of us." Jenna responded.

"I am done with both of you." Carissa cut in before either of us could say another word.

Walking toward the arched opening, the light emanating all around us made me squint my eyes. Crossing the threshold, I had to raise my hand up to help further shield myself. The moment we were through I could no longer move. The rest took several more steps before realizing I was not at their side.

"Come on." Alexander demanded annoyed.

"Would if I could dear brother. Seems this is as far as I am permitted to go."

"He isn't worthy." A deep voice boomed around us. The same lilt to his voice as my Beauty's.

"The fuck?" I blurted.

Carissa was at my side, fear in her eyes as they shifted from me to survey the room then back. Damn her. Part of me wanted to reach out to brush the hair that fell loosely in front of her eyes while the other wanted to shove her away.

"We can't leave him." Carissa sounded frantic.

"Beauty, you need to see this through. I will be right here waiting for you when you get back." I laughed.

"This could be another..." Carissa didn't get to finish her sentence. At least not that I got to hear.

He was gone. Vanished right before our eyes. One moment I was close enough to smell his cologne, the next had a breeze stealing the scent away with him. He seemed to float away on petals in the wind. Up in a swirl until we could no longer see him.

"Where is he?" Jenna cut through the sob that I realized was coming from me.

"That depends on the rest of you. Succeed and you will have to choose his fate." The voice sounded nearby.

"I am so sick of that fucking word." Jenna's anger was evident.

"Then proceed." The voice held a mocking tone this time as if she amused it.

I suddenly wished the owner would step forward to face her. I wanted her to lash out all her pent-up rage before I surrendered to the anger bubbling up within.

"This isn't helping him. Let's go." Alexander's words were even but the glassy look in his eyes gave him away.

"Ok." It was all I could manage to say.

We stepped further in. The light dimmed to allow us the opportunity to really see where we were. The floor was a mixture of light grey and dusty blue tiles. The blue tiles were placed to create a large lily that was centered in the room. The tiled petals held a soft calming glow to them making my ire lower. Lifting my head, I took in the pale grey walls with six smooth columns perfectly aligned around the circular room. The ceiling did not exist. Clouds floated on the subtle wind we could feel around us.

Jenna moved to the very center of the room. Spinning slowly in place, I knew her well enough to know she was memorizing every detail. A silent search for exits, for places others could hide, for any dangers that may wait. Only I saw nothing. Smooth walls never broke for a door or hallway. No ledges rested above us. No windows existed to let the light that had blinded us in.

"This is where your final trial will take place. These two shall be your witness. Their lives as well as the other's life, will depend on you." Our unknown host spoke.

"Then bring it the fuck on, you lucky charms bastard." Jenna raised her arms, hands daring him to come to her with a wag of her fingers.

CHAPTER 14
~ JENNA ~

This fucker was pissing me off to no end. This had to be the ultimate reason no one was known for returning. Obviously, some had though at some point and that is what I held on to for strength. I was reminded of a bully enjoying toying with those they felt were beneath them or weaker than them. If I was right, I really wanted them to step out from where they were hiding.

"Well?" I practically yelled.

No further taunting was needed. My head spun, everything faded into darkness. The sound of a river reached my ears. Gentle water washing over rocks with a steady rhythm. A few birds could be heard overhead, with the aroma of fresh bread wafting around. A smile tugged at my lips. A sense of peace replaced the constant state of alarm. Was I dead? Was this Heaven? A voice in my head told me to just stay here like this and let it all go. I couldn't. The faces of those counting on me flashed in my mind forcing me to look.

The sun was so bright that I lifted my hand for shade, only a larger shadow moved the moment I did. Hazy, the silhouette slowly came into focus and had me shooting straight up while searching for a weapon.

"Woah, what's wrong?" he asked so calmly that I had to blink a couple times to make sure it was really him.

"What are you doing here, Jack?"

"Jack?" His brow furrowed, his hands pushing off the ground as he moved to stand.

"Yes, Jackass. What is going on? Did you set this up? I am so fucking stupid. It is all clicking into place. You're the asshole that wanted Vanessa to tell me who I am."

"Vanessa?" He took a step forward as if he wanted to hold me but stopped when I raised my hands.

"Eve, you are not making any sense. What has taken hold of you? Is this his doing? Has Adam done something?"

I swallowed hard. The knowledge stealing my breath. Death. Jack. Salazar. That was why he wanted me back. The jackass, Death was or rather is, Salazar. This answered so many questions that had been taking up residence in my brain.

"No." I said softly.

"Then tell me." His voice was so much softer than when we spoke before.

Eyeing him carefully, I felt that same pull that had me screwing him in the bathroom. Something in this man did call to something in me. Now I knew why. If I was even a small part of Eve, of course I am going to be drawn to the man she gave her life to be with. Why did he not just tell me he was Salazar though? Why the charade of "Mr. No Name"? Something was still missing. Was he worried that she or rather I would blame him for being killed? I suppose that would be within her rights to resent him. Her? Mine? Fuck this was confusing.

"Why are you here?"

"Whatever do you mean, my Missing Piece?"

Fuck if those words didn't stir something within me. Internally I reminded myself of the casual way he dispatched others for years and that it appeared now, he was the one who put the hit on the Fates.

"Salazar" His name felt familiar and foreign on my tongue, "why are we together? What is it you want from me?"

If this was a memory we could interact with, then I would get to the root of all my misery.

"I have lived so long. Most of my life, I did not know my purpose here. Still, the need alludes me in truth. Always alone. Always wandering. I was a part of the world changing around me but never belonged to it. Not until I saw you. Something about you filled in that void I could not name. You are the piece I needed to be whole. For this reason, I will always keep you safe. I will always be there for you and provide all that you desire. I cannot be without you again."

"If you were to lose me?" I let his arms slip around my waist to pull me close.

"I would torture those that took you from me no matter if they be Gods or men. I would make them feel the pain I would feel until they gave you back to me. They would suffer far worse than any have ever suffered before or would again."

His eyes swirled black with that same glowing white I was all too familiar with. He suddenly took a step back with a snarl.

"Why do I see pain in you? Suffering? Rage?" His hands came back to grip my arms tight.

"You failed. You didn't keep your word to her. To me. You were too late." I felt a tear slip down my cheek at the horror filling his eyes which returned to the brilliant blue hue.

"I will make it right." I heard him say just before I was swept away on a current of time.

I was everywhere and nowhere. A scene playing out before me like a play. A young woman sat at a grave crying. Her face hidden in her hands muffling the sobs that shook her whole body. I looked down at her, straining to hear the words broken by her sorrow.

"Mother, I wish you were here. I, I don't know what to do." She tried to wipe the tears away from her reddened cheeks.

"Mother?" I questioned. She was so much younger, but she was unmistakable. My grandmother had passed long before I was born but I know that they had been close. Mother had told me many stories about her.

"I wish for a child of my own, yet it seems that God has abandoned me. No matter my prayers, they remain unanswered. I yearn for a daughter that I can raise as you raised me. To pass on the love you showed me. Oh mother, what have I done to deserve such a barren existence?"

"Nothing." A deep male voice responded causing my mother to topple to the side when she turned.

"Who are you? Do not come near or I shall scream."

"I am here to answer your prayers." He confided.

My mother's fear had her rushing to her feet to run away. A single hand on her shoulder halted her escape. She turned to face him as a warm glow radiated from his eyes. He was assessing her, laying judgment.

"Yes, you will do nicely. I can assure that you and your husband will be blessed with a child this night if we can come to terms. You will give birth to a girl. Raise her to be a worthy lady as you desire."

"What do you want in return?" My mother's voice shook in response, yet she did not continue her attempts to flee.

"Her. When she is an adult of age. I will come for her. She will have the choice to come with me, which I assure you she will. When I do, you will not interfere. You will tell no one of our arrangement as well.”

“What if she does not want to accompany you? What if I refuse to let her leave?”

“Then you, your husband, and all those you hold dear will perish. I can assure you; she will want to come to me.”

I could see the war raging within her. The desire for a child was so great it outweighed the looming fear of his intentions. Her fingers fidgeted nervously for several minutes before she nodded. In response, he grinned wide.

“Go home then and congratulations to you on becoming a mother.”

So that was all it had taken. My mother wanted a child so badly that she agreed to let a stranger attempt to take me. Was she really so certain I would not have gone with him? This was making my head spin for more than the whirlwind that continued to pull me from one time to the next.

Landing, after small glimpses of my childhood, in a dark room lit by candles. I saw my mother seated at a table with 4 others. They all held hands and immediately I knew what I was witnessing. An older woman I did not know sat with a black veil over her face. Her voice the only one to call out in what sounded like a Romanian accent.

“Spirits. We ask that you help us in our time of need. Mrs. Devereaux has been searching for years without answers. Does one wait in the shadows to take her dear daughter?”

“Yes.” I spoke on impulse.

The woman jerked in shock, quickly clearing her throat to cover. I knew she had heard me though. I wanted to tell her to tell my mother not to let me go home that night but deep inside I knew it was futile. Somehow, some way, this was always meant to happen.

"Spirit, can she stop this man from taking Jenna?"

"He will not be the one to take her." I spoke truthfully.

She repeated all I said to my mother who began to cry in relief before she asked her who would take me. Not waiting for the veiled woman to ask, I replied.

"Tell her that her daughter will always love her very much. Tell Mrs. Devereaux that she doesn't need to worry. Jenna will be fine. She raised a strong woman."

I couldn't stop the tears that fell from my eyes. My mother would think I died, that I wasn't fine. Yet if I could give her some peace for a short time, I would. She had tried to find a way to stop something no longer in her control. Wanting to protect me from a deal she had made only caused me to miss her. I watched her completely break down on hearing my words. Her sorrow made me take a step towards her.

Another torrent of air brought me to the center of several times at once. My mother and father falling apart after my departure to the convent, the nun arriving at the convent to discover all of the lifeless bodies I left behind, Marcus' fight to leave the Vatican and subsequent confession to the night sky of missing me, Salazar holding Eve's cold body in his arms when Adam appears. They spun around me, each cry in pain or anger clear to my ears. The sound rose until it was deafening. My hands flew up in an attempt to silence the noise even as my knees buckled.

This was the aftermath of my existence. Every word burying me. Every cry slicing my flesh. Then a whisper began to filter into the madness. My ears strained to hear it. Salvation clawing at me to listen.

"Jenna, you are so much more. Think. Remember those you helped. Those you will help. The innocent people that need you. Their champion." Carissa's voice pleaded.

"Damn it, you leech. Fucking stop being a little bitch and fight back. It's what you do." Azrael demanded.

As much as he pissed me off, it bolstered my resolve even more than my friend. That word remained strange to me, but it was true. Carissa was my friend, and my friend needed me to get off my ass.

A primal scream tore from my chest. At once I stood, my wings spreading out to cast off the memory lane trip once and for all. I was back at the center of the room. The cuts I had felt were healing on my arms, legs, and back.

"You really were trying to kill me." I said while I assessed the injuries.

"No. We were simply making sure you were strong enough." The voice came from behind.

I turned to see a man, grey hair with salt and pepper stubble, liquid silver eyes staring straight into my own. He wore black pants with a grey T-shirt that showed a muscular body underneath. What made me chuckle a little was the realization that he was barefoot.

"Who are you?" I asked.

"I have had a lot of names over the years and even more looks. I take the form of whatever is needed for those that deserve my attention."

"I am so over all the cryptic shit. What should we call you?"

"Zeus. Cernunnos. Baphomet. Anubis." He shrugged.

"Got it. You're a God." I shook my head, the others joining me at the center.

"Where is Azrael?" Carissa demanded.

With a wave of his hand, the petals appeared above slowly drifting down to form the missing McKenzie.

"So, what now?" Alexander asked with obvious relief.

"Now? Well, that is entirely up to her. I can give her the book and she can leave with it, or..." He paused to look at the four of us, "I can tell you each one thing to assist you in your future and you can all leave. The choice rests with her."

"Great. We're fucked." Azrael exclaimed.

If it had been just me and the brothers, I might have been able to do it. Carissa was a different story. I would never be able to face Joanna if I left her daughter here.

"We are all going home." I finally confirmed.

"Lovely." He smiled, "Carissa, you're first. Then Azrael, Alexander, and finally you."

He stepped to Carissa, whispering in her ear so low even I couldn't hear. She appeared to glow all around by the time he was done then shimmered into nothing. Stepping to Azrael, he didn't lean in or try to hide his words.

"You fight against what is destined. Fight too long and your destiny will rot, with it, your life. You are not worthy, but you know that better than anyone." He ended and immediately Azrael was gone without notice.

"Alexander, you are worthy of your future, but you are too prideful. You will have to learn to set aside yourself if you wish to survive what you have set in motion. Balance must be maintained." Alexander opened his mouth to reply but disappeared before he could utter a syllable.

"Jenna. My dear Jenna. Your very existence causes an unbalance in the natural order. I do wish I could offer something to help you in all that will befall you. A balance must be found for you as well. This is the way of things. Open yourself up to those you trust. It is the only way you will ever find the purpose and peace you desire so badly. You have more allies than you realize. The universe as you like to say isn't through *fucking* with you.

With that, he too was gone. The blue lily at my feet began to shimmer, a sight I bore witness to briefly then I was back in the garden.

"This babysitting shit is for the ghouls. I could even summon a reaper here to do my bidding if we didn't have to stay in Goldilocks' castle." Another dagger embedded in the wall.

"We will know soon enough if they were successful." Vanessa offered.

"Lovely. Maybe I'll get lucky, and the whiney bitch won't make it back." I smirked.

Vanessa sighed heavily, her attention returning to the assortment of dishes Joanna had sent for us. Seemed my little Trinket had never sampled a lot of things in life. Her innocence made me nauseous. I had never spent this much time with anyone, not even in Hell. Well except for Lucifer. He was the only one I ever had around for long periods and those were usually training or satisfying his every sadistic need.

He seemed to get real pleasure from using me or when in his worst moods, watching me torture others. Hell was quite the place to grow up. Which is I suppose why I was always special.

Most demons just were. They would pop into existence from some demented person's death or a purgatory soul that became so enraged redemption was off the table. I was a baby given to other demons to tend till I came of age. Even in my childhood I was trained by every manner of vile soul that passed through our gates. When I stopped aging, I began sessions with Lucifer himself.

My first lesson almost killed me. The excitement of a stronger opponent erased any fear I held. Lucifer began by testing my skills with a sword, my hand-to-hand combat skills in a mixture of forms practiced all over the world, then into my understanding of the human condition. To entice or trap a soul, one needed to understand them. I was bleeding out while standing still to answer every question he had. I collapsed to the floor only to wake up in a bed that was not mine.

A demon sat beside me on the bed cleaning my wounds. He had horns like mine, whereas mine were shiny black that curved without curling around, his curled reminding me of a ram. It was the only time I ever saw anyone with horns that were also shiny black. Lucifer entered, noticed me staring up at his horns and cut them from his head without a second thought.

"Here." He had said. "A gift for doing well in your studies."

The demon continued cleaning up as if nothing had happened, even as black blood began seeping down his head to his shoulders. I never did see the demon again after that. Lucifer had come to sit on the bed, roughly turning my face to see how I was healing. Satisfied he stood and moved away.

"Get up and strip." He commanded.

"I'm ok." I grumbled; hating being told what to do even by the Devil himself.

"I won't repeat myself."

Looking at the horns by my feet, I got up from the bed. A smirk curled the side of my lips, my hand reaching up to tear my top from my body. Not wasting any time, I set my body afire to disintegrate the rest of the clothes I wore. Under my feet, the rubber of my shoes still bubbled when I took a step forward.

That was all it took, one arm hooked around my waist, my body brought flush to his as he too let fire remove the fabric he wore. There was nothing soft about his lips on mine. Rough, bruising kisses trailed from my mouth down my neck to my collarbone. Nips of teeth joined in the path up my neck to my ear.

I could feel his massive length trapped between our bodies one heartbeat then shoving deep inside my body the next. I screamed in pain and pleasure. My legs wrapped around him, his hands demanding on my hips to match the speed of each thrust. Falling backwards onto the bed, he didn't stop. His legs coming up to force mine to spread wide. Mouth capturing my breast, he bit my nipple sending a wave of pleasure through every nerve.

His hips pulled back then slammed his cock deep, my body clenching around him looking for release. Suddenly slowing a little, I felt his hands shift to grab my ass, with a firm grip, he used me. I was his. He was not just the ruler of Hell, but he was my Master. Relishing the feel of him filling me, his mouth sucking on my breasts, I came hard when I felt him drive one of his fingers into my ass. He worked his finger, fucking me in each at the same time.

The delicious torment was all consuming. His other hand squeezed my breast, his mouth moving back up my neck to claim mine. The moment his tongue pushed inside, I felt something else replace his finger going further into ass. My nails clawed down his back, my moan smothered between the tangle of tongues and lips. I let myself go, my body shaking as waves of pleasure shot through every limb to leave me craving more.

He did not relent. Pulling free of me, he yanked me up till I was on all fours near the edge of the bed. This time, his dick claimed my ass and the tail I caught a glimpse of slammed into my cunt. Holding onto my hips, he rode me harder making me grip the bed and fight to keep from falling forward. I swore under my breath, sweat coating every inch of my flesh. He leaned forward licking where my wings resided, and I knew it was not a request. Letting them unfurl, he took hold painfully pulling me up while never slowing his thrusts.

Arching back, he shouted with his release, hips pumping until he was spent. There was no clean up or tenderness after. He stepped away already fully dressed and completely human looking by the time I slid from the mattress. My body hummed, adrenaline coursing in my veins with an edge that begged for more. Not necessarily more sex, but more of something.

"Change." He stated and I obeyed. Gone were my wings, my horns ceased to protrude from the top of my head, and my skin became that pinkish hue of humans. At the time, only a couple of tattoos adorned my skin.

"I want you to go kill the Grand Coven Leader over all the lands except this continent." He pointed to a map that appeared as his hand raised.

I nodded knowing that they were the most powerful of all the warlocks. This was a mission and a test. One that if I failed and survived, I may as well end my existence because he would.

How long ago had that been? The years all rolled together. I never even got to kill them all when he dragged me back to Hell. He said the goal was accomplished, whatever the Heaven that meant. I did learn of The Agora back then. That's when I first met Goldilocks' family. I'm not sure what rubs me so wrong about her, but I wish some bear shifters would devour her just to give me a smile.

"What is so funny?" Vanessa interrupted my thoughts with her timid little voice.

"Scuse me?" I threw a dagger in her direction, narrowly missing her head to land in the chair. She didn't even flinch.

"Gotta say, you are an interesting little Trinket."

"Vanessa." She corrected me.

I moved, leaning over her so close she had to lean back. I smirked and tapped the tip of the dagger I yanked from the chair to her lips.

"Trinket. See that's all you are to me. You may be some big deal Fate, but to me.... You're my little trinket even if that vamp technically owns you now."

CHAPTER 16
~ SALAZAR ~

I appeared in the hallway of The Agora with a wince. I knew since she had become close with them that I would likely need to make myself known here eventually. Other than the souls in what many refer to as Purgatory, I have not spent much time in the company of people. I had also never before set foot inside this place. Many seemed to recognize what I was, or at least a hint at my nature. They moved away, clearing a path for any direction they thought I may take. The large inky black wings may have had a hand in revealing my identity.

In truth, I was attempting to contain myself. A testament to the level of patience I can pretend to have when everything in me was screaming to go to her. I spotted what I knew to be Joanna first. Just because I never ventured out did not mean I didn't keep tabs on those of importance. She stopped in her tracks when her eyes locked with mine. At once I knew she had been coming to collect me but still held doubts until that moment.

My desire to hasten the events had me walking to her, my hand outstretched in greeting when I neared. She glanced from the appendage back to me then down again. Tentatively, she shook my hand then forced a small smile to her face.

"Jack... I mean Death." She fumbled.

"Salazar." I corrected only to witness her jaw go slack.

Mouth agape, she stood there staring at me while I simply raised a brow. Obviously, she knew my name and my relationship with Eve. One of my servants had informed me the Fate was here and of the little mission she had sent my Missing Piece on. When surrounded by the recently deceased, nothing remained secret for long. The only unknown for me was Jenna's exact location. When here, my connection to her was always hazy. While she was at the caverns, it had been completely severed.

Now I felt a faint pull toward her but refused to do something to anger my Missing Piece. We were so close. I had waited, planned, acted to find her and return her into being. Nothing would take her from me this time. When I was about to snap her out of her daze, a fist landed across my jaw sending rage through me. Black wings expanded behind me as I moved to see who had dared strike me. Only when the brown hues I knew better than my own gaze fixed on mine, I immediately softened.

"You asshole!" Jenna cursed, going for another blow but I caught her wrist this time and wrapped her in my arms.

"My office might be the best place for this reunion." Carissa urged from beside her, ushering us down the hall with a nod to her mother.

I reluctantly released her and followed. Silence reigned until we were safely behind closed doors. Jenna paced like an animal in a cage. Studying those bars for the best time to strike.

The look she was giving me sent a shiver of guilt as well as excitement through me. She was mad but she knew. Better yet, she believed.

"Explain. Both of you." Carissa cut her eyes between us expectantly.

"You already know about Death aka Jackass. Well turns out he has another name... Salazar." Jenna filled in the blanks she apparently had not yet shared with the younger Ms. Thomas.

Carissa's eyes went wide, her gaze looking up from my black boots to my black jeans with fitted black t-shirt. I had considered wearing something in a different color because of what Jenna had said before but I was comfortable in this.

"She is telling the truth. Not that you should have any reason to doubt her. I brought her back, Eve back, for selfish reasons but now even more than that. She is needed by more than me." I confessed.

"Vanessa didn't say shit about that. Just me needing to discover who I was by looking at my past life. She said I needed to do that...." Jenna's voice trailed off, the remaining words slipping out on a whisper, "if I wanted to win this time."

"We can do it. Together." I told her. I had known there would be repercussions but as of yet, I wasn't entirely sure what they were going to be. The only thing I knew to be absolute was us beating the odds if we were as one. Centuries ago, I hadn't known there was a battle being waged dependent on us, now I knew. Now she knew. And this time, things would be very different.

When I thought things couldn't get worse, a letter arrived out of thin air to land on Carissa's desk. A deep red envelope with a black note inside. I couldn't help but laugh at the lack of originality. Then again, tradition as old as anyone can recall is what the Elders believed in and upheld with dire consequences. I was only marginally surprised when Joanna and Carissa informed the rest of us about the summons.

They required an audience with me and Salazar. The part related to me was more the demand while when mentioning him, it was a request. Shunned by them for hundreds of years and now they want to act like I owe them. I was damn ready to speak with them face to face.

The unfortunate part was their assertion this meeting take place here at The Agora. Apparently, they had a special room on the grounds for similar occasions where, I discovered, they expected those attending to dress formally. Good fucking luck with that.

Showing up in a pair of blue jeans with brown boots and a white tank topped off with a short tan sweater, I strolled in casually. I would not bow to them no matter what they had to say. Each stood on a raised platform, a banner high overhead with the symbol for each of their houses. Each banner was red with the symbol in a black shimmering thread. We stood in silence, the delay allowing me to study the fitted suits the men wore and the elegantly beaded gowns on the women at their sides. None stood alone which I found strange.

Walking in several minutes late, he moved to stand beside me. For the first time, he wore something other than all black. Though the dress shoes, pants, and jacket were black. The shirt he wore was crisp white. I couldn't help but roll my eyes at his acquiescence.

"Ms. Devereaux, it has been brought to our attention that your heritage has at last been confirmed. While you remain an abomination, the Elders do acknowledge you and your place in our society."

"Gee, I'm so fucking honored by your acceptance. I shall at last be able to sleep peacefully tucked into my little bed. Ever the *abomination* and ever ready to show you personally what that really means. Of course, we can also agree to leave each other the fuck alone too." I didn't even try to hide the snarky tone from my voice. Their eyes narrowing in disdain before turning to him as if I hadn't uttered a word.

"Salazar, we long thought you lost to time. Perhaps even succumbed to your own death as it were. We want to take this opportunity to offer our hand in friendship. Perhaps even in solidarity at whatever may be coming." They all smiled in response with nods of approval, including the Jackass. So, when he spoke, I was surprised.

"Friendship? How would I accept the friendship of those

that hold her in such contempt? You may take your offer and never trouble her or me again if you wish to remain the immortals you believe yourselves to be. Do otherwise if you wish to test what Death really means to each of you." His voice never rose, every word coming out as if he were engaged in a pleasant conversation which only made him seem more deadly.

Nodding when he finished, he grabbed my hand, a laugh erupting from my chest at the blanched expressions they wore as we left without waiting another moment. They thought I was disrespectful and a mistake. I had to wonder what they were thinking after that little display.

For the first time, I felt a real crack in the walls I kept up around him. The pull he held beginning to fracture my resolve. I saw a glimpse of what Eve must have seen in him and I wondered if he saw who I am now or if he only saw her. Did I really care? Making him stop, I yanked my hand from his.

"I'm not her. I know I have her essence or soul or energy or whatever the fuck, but I am not the woman you knew. I won't pretend to be her either. Not looking for a prince to come rescue me or anyone to see me through. Perfectly capable on my own and I don't need you." I confessed.

"I know. She didn't need me either. I needed her. I need you. You see, Jenna, that is the biggest attraction you hold. You don't need anyone which means you chose me every day over and over till you were taken from me. I know you will continue to choose me too in time. You know who I am and what I am. There are no more secrets between us. All I want is you." He took a step closer till I was forced to tilt my head up to meet his intense stare.

"Fucking hell." I muttered. "You can't go around saying things like that. It's confusing enough as it is. You said before that there was more, and Vanessa said there is something I will have to fight for or against. You even said I was important to more than just you. So, what the hell was that supposed to mean?"

"I admit I offset the balance by bringing you back. There will be consequences. Dire ones given what I did. There is no way that this will not spill into the mortal world as well as our own. I was warned just how bad this would be and I did it anyway. I would do it again too. So yes, you are important to a lot of people."

"You really that desperate? I was gone for what? Hundreds of years? Thousands? And you couldn't find anyone else? For fuck's sake, what is *wrong* with you? Eve fuck your world up that bad?" I looked up at him exasperated.

"They weren't you." He gripped my elbows in his hands tightly. His own frustration at my refusal to blindly accept all this seeping out.

CHAPTER 18
~ SALAZAR ~

"Why do you fight me at every turn? Why must you be so damn stubborn? I will always do whatever I must to bring you back to me no matter how long it takes. I am not whole without you. Only the promise of your return has kept me from turning every last mortal to dust." I did my best to keep my cool, but I was hanging on by a thread, a very thin fucking thread.

"So, you thought you would bring her back to you and what? You would live happily ever after. What is with the men in my life treating others so casually? Perhaps no one told you this when you popped into existence, but killing people for no good reason is not the way to win a woman's heart." She stopped to study me; only then did I realize that my eyes had turned black.

"*Men.*" I spat the word out as if doing so could eliminate it from my thoughts. "Do you still harbor feelings for Marcus? Do **not** lie to me."

Anyone else would cower before me when I was angered.

Not my Missing Piece, she squared her shoulders to stand as tall as her stature would allow and held my gaze. If she only knew how much of Eve's spirit was shown through her every defiance. She would. Learning what she had, seeing that glimpse, it was all that was needed to open the doorway to her past. She would slowly remember everything if she didn't already. No one had exactly done what I had before. We were in uncharted waters.

"Marcus and I spent centuries together. That should tell you all you need to know." Jenna offered in a tone I recognized as final.

"Give me a chance and I will erase all those petty feelings you think you have for him. I know you sense the connection we share. The love unending between us. You are mine and I am yours. The sooner you accept it, the sooner..." She cut me off.

"The sooner what? I can join you in killing. I can help you face whatever Hell you've unleashed on the world. I can be yours without a damn choice like some mindless damsel in some boring romance novel, instantly in love because of destiny. Am I supposed to fall into your arms, forget the plans I had for my own life, my own choices?" Jenna was furious but the fury in her eyes only made me want to pull her near.

"You've already started. Both of you have in fact." Vanessa startled the both of us.

We had been so engrossed in our discussion that we hadn't sensed the Fate enter. Nor the two women now standing behind her looking apprehensive. I recognized her golden eyes, red hair, and alabaster skin. The Fate would be known to any that paid attention. Only doubt of actually seeing a Fate would keep them from uttering a word in confirmation. She looked on as if we were in the midst of a normal conversation. The absurdity stealing some of the tension from within.

"What the fuck are you on about now?" Jenna moved toward the trio.

"Since the day of your birth, E...Jenna," Vanessa continued, "the balance has been shifting around you. Little moments. Big moments. Even your run in with Victor. The scales were trying to see how much of a shift was needed."

"Things I would have learned from your book no doubt." Jenna stated on a huff.

"Oh, you were never going to actually get the book." Vanessa confirmed and Jenna shot her eyes toward her with a look that said she was on the edge of losing her restraint.

"The fuck?" Jenna seemed unable to say more.

"It was necessary. I knew that you would never leave them all behind though." Vanessa replied so nonchalantly I wanted to laugh.

"Is she whole now?" I interjected.

"Not yet. She will be. There are a few things she has yet to remember." The Fate answered.

"How long do you think it will be before she remembers everything?" I asked.

"Not long now. She fights against it, but she cannot stop it." Vanessa confirmed.

"Hello? *SHE* is right fucking here." Jenna stepped closer.

"We know." Vanessa spoke first, no hint of understanding in her voice.

CHAPTER 19
~ JENNA ~

"I need to go. All this. You." I pointed at Jack, Salazar, whatever the fuck his name is.

Right now, my brain was on overload. I barely had time to adjust to the news that I was the reincarnation of Eve. Eve from the Bible story. From the garden. The creation of all mankind if you followed that faith. And I had. I was raised to believe. My wedding was planned in my head the moment I fell in awe of Trent, complete with the walk down the aisle in the same church I was baptized in.

Shaking my head, I pushed past everyone to walk through the first door I found. Gone was The Agora in favor of my apartment. I kept moving until I stood in the middle of my living room. The frustration bubbling up sent my arms out to my sides, wings smashing into the table, vase, and mirror as a scream ripped free. Long and loud, releasing some of the pent-up pressure, I collapsed to the ground when I could no longer sustain the outburst. Sitting in a lump on the floor, I vaguely felt thankful for the witch's barrier encasing my home.

The mirror lay in shards around me, my wings stretching out before wrapping around my body. I sat there in my cocoon, fingers reaching up to stroke the feathers surrounding me. It was the first time I'd ever really studied them. Faintly I was aware of the drips falling onto my feet and legs. When was the last time I really cried? Not a sorrowful moment but a soul cleansing release?

A soft glow gained strength until I had to close my eyes. The moment darkness ruled, everything clicked into place. Eve's life played out all at once, yet I felt every moment as if it just happened. Salazar was unmistakable in her life. True happiness filled Eve's heart, with him she found peace. She was going to leave with him. Abandon her home to spend the rest of her days with the man who was not a man at all. If only she had rushed back to tell him when she had made her choice. Maybe she would have lived, and my life wouldn't be a fucking shit show from Hell.

I reflected on everything I have learned since my initiation into the world beyond. There were so many different kinds of people in the world. No longer did I see them as monsters, but as people who were just trying to live their lives. I was a vampire, then I was also Death, then my energy was that of a woman who had enough impact to have a story written about her in the Bible. The motherfucking bible.

He had fallen in love with her. In all the time since, how could he not have moved on? Seriously, what kind of psycho was I dealing with? Killing the Fates had been nothing to him. Killing those that had crossed my path when I thought I was mortal seemed to have given him a sense of satisfaction. He is Death, the Angel of Death to be specific. Yet shouldn't that teach him the value of life?

"Fuck. Fuck. Fuck." The word fell from my lips. I felt like a victim, with no sense of control over my life, my future being directed by others with the expectation I follow along.

"No." I stood abruptly.

I was not going to blindly proceed. There was always a choice to be made. Fate can throw shit in my path but how I respond is up to me. Not to mention what this was going to do to the rest of the world. Vanessa and Salazar said this would spill into the mortal realm. To be the cause of another's suffering did not sit well with me.

A heavy sigh was the last act allowed. The broom my weapon of choice to begin bringing order back to my life. Meticulously, I swept up the mess I had made. The broken furniture was picked up and taken to the garbage chute. Walking back into my apartment, I paused to survey the area. Everything was back in place, although a few things were now missing. Perhaps a remodel was in order anyway.

Closing the door behind me, there was no surprise when I heard another door open and close. Carissa entered cautiously, her gaze darting around likely looking for the carnage now gone. When at last she found me, she visibly relaxed. Moving more confidently, she came to sit at the island in the kitchen area. Neither of us spoke, instead I grabbed a bottle of vodka, Carissa's preferred alcohol and poured two glasses.

Sliding one to her, I stood on the other side sipping the clear liquid while I gave her time to start. I had nothing to really say to anyone. She meanwhile turned the glass around in her hands before taking her first drink. Her eyes dropped to counter, the glass swirling the fluid longer before she shot the remainder down and slid the glass back to me. With a raised brow, I filled it a bit higher this time. Three more times we played out this little act till I could no longer keep silent.

"Oh, for fuck's sake. This isn't a first date or a hotel room after prom. Say what you want to say, Carissa."

"Must you be so crass?" Carissa sighed.

"Yes." I stated curtly.

"I wanted to make sure you were ok. You've been through a lot and..." Her lip caught between her teeth.

"And you want to discuss the difference I tasted in your blood privately." I surmised.

Carissa rose to pace between the kitchen and living room. I knew from the moment I had tasted the first drop of her blood; we would need to have a conversation. The way I healed, the energy I felt course through my veins, the fear I saw in her eyes despite her determination to help me.

Grabbing the bottle, I moved to the couch. My hand motioned for her to join me either on the couch or the chair nearby. She took her time settling into the seat across from me. Her hands kept rolling the glass between her palms. I studied the tension she appeared to hold in every muscle. I've seen her unsure numerous times before, but this was different. She was not simply on edge, she was scared.

"Jenna, what I did in letting you drink from me is forbidden. My family has rules we have always followed for very good reason."

"As servants to the Host of The Agora?" I raised a brow.

"Something like that." She nodded.

Carissa was not an ordinary human. I could say that now without any doubt. What I could not say however, was what she was. None of the training Marcus had provided ever tasted like hers. Seems I was not the only one who was unique or kept secrets.

"You're not going to tell me though, are you." I stated.

"I can't. At least not now. Besides, I think you have enough on your plate. You have found out all you are and let's not forget, you have a demon's life in your hands." Carissa raised her brow, her head tilting slightly.

"Yes, the fucking fire demon. Lucifer's own Gods damn fire no less. What the hell am I going to do with her? I don't know why I didn't just end her in the arena. Guess she just warmed my cold dead heart." I laughed without any joy.

"How the hell did my life go tits up so spectacularly? Fucking Death..." my words were stalled when Carissa cut in with an honest laugh.

"Literally." She laughed harder when my eyes widened, and I lost myself joining her.

"I will absolutely not apologize for it either. The man has a pull I can't deny. Plus, he is pleasantly blessed downstairs." I smirked around the rim of my glass as I took a sip.

"Sex and death in general. Two things you have certainly not shied from since I have known you. Though you use others for pleasure without any connection. Don't you get lonely?" Carissa's voice raised the question while her eyes answered on her behalf.

"I have spent these years not knowing who the fuck I was. Add to that how I even became a vampire then how things turned out with Marcus... I would say I've been better off on my own. No one can let you down if you don't depend on them." I sighed.

Carissa looked down, defeated in my response as if she hoped my answer may provide clarity for something else. She was a friend. One, I realized, I wanted to keep. The problem is my lack of practice. Centuries had passed since I had a true friend. Marcus did not count given our relationship. How did one show support or offer comfort? *Shit.*

"Look, I suck at this shit like a nun on her knees. You're going to have to help me here. We stuck a fucking spear in the whole what you are topic but something else is up. I'll listen if that is what you need or try to offer advice. Just let it out." I leaned forward to meet her gaze.

She sighed, offering her glass to me for a refill. Her chest and cheeks were already flushed from the alcohol. Liquid courage apparently was what she sought now.

"Despite the description, you are doing fine. It's just something I am not sure how to even put into words." She nibbled her lower lip.

"Who is he? Or she? Or them?"

"That is just it. There is no one. Every man I have dated has felt wrong and I have never felt an attraction to a woman. What if I am meant to be alone?" Carissa's voice softened to a whisper.

"Carissa, you're smoking hot. I would take you to bed if it wouldn't make things weird and you were into it. You're thinking too much about this. Now I know what I am about to ask will likely piss in your Cheerios but...what about that asshole, Azrael?" I saw her flinch as soon as his name left my lips.

"He will never share my values. Any man that takes my heart must be approved by the Host and I cannot see Azrael measuring up. Whenever he touches me, I feel a strange sensation spread throughout my body. It's almost like an electrical current." She held the glass in one hand to rub the other up and down her arm in memory.

"That's a new one. Never thought of him as having an electric personality." I teased.

"Shocking, I know." She retorted with a soft smile.

"She has jokes now. She must be feeling more relaxed. One day I will completely shatter that guard you keep up." I teased.

"Trying to make me into someone who feels the need to curse fluently has been a game you've been losing since we met." Her smile was more genuine this time.

Silence fell over us like a warm blanket. There was no anxiety or need to fill the space that hung open. We drank, letting time pass to arrange our thoughts. Each of us had more going on than I realized. So caught up in the shit show of my days, I hadn't noticed Carissa was fighting her own battle.

"Jenna, thank you. For, you know, not pushing things. There are reasons I cannot say more. Same reasons why after what happened, I began thinking of my future. We could have been lost in those caverns. Heck, you got impaled. I saw Azrael flicker out of existence. The temptation to stay in the memory to learn more was almost irresistible. I felt the pull of it. Timing was on our side which is why I believe the Fate wanted us all to go. Only with all of us could we keep from losing ourselves." Carissa met my gaze straight on.

"Ah, so that is what brought on the woe is me. I'll die without ever experiencing a huge cock fear." I teased.

"I'm not a virgin." Carissa blurted.

"You have said that before but sometimes I really wonder. You're missing out if you are. In all honesty though, babe, you are not going to be alone. Prince Charming will come riding up in a white Jeep Wrangler, toss you in and you will drive off with your hair blowing in the wind." I assured her.

"Jeep Wrangler, huh?" She arched a brow.

"Absofuckinglutely. I know there is a little wild in you somewhere. Not overly so but a few sharp edges." I smirked.

"I suppose a few wouldn't hurt. Especially when I have to

deal with Death, a fire demon, a Fate, and a woman who scares them all." Carissa raised her glass in a toast.

Tapping my glass to hers, I realized I really was not alone and never would be again.

CHAPTER 20
~ ADEMIA ~

"This sucks Cerberus' sweaty balls. I cannot stay in this Goldilocks' prison forever. There is too much goodness and far too many rules." I snarled as I plopped into the black tufted chair.

The room around me was one designed for those of a darker nature on their visits to The Agora. Comfortable enough but could not hide the truth of where we were. Currently no one else inhabited the space. One small favor as my mood was sour enough. Dealing with others when my flames were bound by the Host would be torture.

Needing to blow off steam, I rose up and made my way to the first door I saw. A smile curled my lips as I looked over the space. Targets were off in the distance at varying points. Almost everything in the room was flammable.

"Perfect." I sighed, flames dancing from fingertips.

The door disappeared, confirmation that no one else would be able to enter unannounced and *accidentally* get hurt by whatever may be going on. Standing at the line with shoulders parallel to the first target shaped like a Lycan, a second ticked away, my hand flying up to send a bolt of fire dead center. Twirling down the lane from one to the next, I dipped then leapt then slid with every shot. Each blow hit its mark with absolute precision. When I was done, the entire back wall was ablaze.

Heat filled the room, sweat beading along my skin to soak in the black pants and loose grey tank top I wore. Every drip that went down the curves of my body sent a thrill through out. This felt like home. The aroma of blood, sweat, tears, and burnt flesh came to mind. I could almost smell each nuance. Faint echos of the past filled my ears: screams, pleas, whimpers, laughter, the crack of whips against flesh.

"Hellfire. I actually miss the place. I miss the damn freedom." I closed my eyes.

Fire outlined my entire body, the fabric that covered me evaporating in an instant. Slowly my skin grew thicker, black horns sprouted from the top of my head just as leathery wings erupted from my back. Small, hooked claws topped off each wing in the same glossy black as the nails on the tips of my fingers and toes. Flames expanded in strength and size until the room was nothing but an inferno.

Walking to watch the furnishings morph from lit forms to blackened ash to diminish into nothingness made my last remaining human façade give way. Switching from brown hues to inky black, my eyes relished the destruction all around. A swirling inferno surrounded me, the floor beneath my feet resembling ripples cascading across a darkened lake. The Agora's magical essence brought forth replacements in an attempt to refurnish the room only to have them meet the same fate.

"Magnifuckinglicent." I whispered.

Embers dying down, the whirlwind of flames ceased its dance until only the faint glow remained. As the orange hue surrendered to the darkness, the room lit from the same unseen source as before. In a wave, the room restored itself from the apocalyptic remnants to the pristine practice area all expected.

Planning to leave in search of a meal, the door swung inward as it came into existence. Standing on the threshold was the main reason for my frustration. She strolled in without a care and did not flinch when the quiet gust of air signaled the door's departure. This chick really did have a set on her. In this room there were no restraints, entering meant you acknowledged anything that might happen to you. Only problem was the forsaken bond that existed now. My life was no longer my own. Even Lucifer did not have as much say before as this bitch does now. Of course, with him I obeyed regardless since torture or death were the only alternatives. Plus, I liked what I did. Killing. Torturing. Darkening the essence of those that thought they were soooo mighty.

"Hello, Bloodsucker. Want to go another round?" I lifted my right hand, flames igniting from the tips of each finger.

"Yeah, yeah, big bad fire demon. I am trembling in my boots. Does this act really work for you? Do people truly run away just because you show them a bit of fire? A bucket of water and what then?" Jenna scoffed.

Man, how this bitch irritated me.

"Just say what the fuck you want and get your scrawny ass out of here." I retorted.

"What the *fuck* I want is for us to settle how things are going to be from now on. I have actual important matters to attend to and don't need to worry about you and your bullshit." She walked closer.

I knew she was trying to show how little she feared me or

anyone for that matter. If I didn't know how she has the disgusting moral streak, I may have thought twice. Instead, I shot a small burst to singe a hole into her blue jeans about mid-thigh then another at her knee on the other leg.

"That's better." I smirked.

"You are a child." She sighed.

"Ademia, I don't have time for your shit so listen carefully. You are now going to assist The Agora. You will have a dwelling set up for you off site but will answer whenever they call. There are tasks best suited for someone like you." She motioned up and down with her hand, an obvious disdain coloring her words.

"You mean someone willing to get dirty. Do the things you and little Goldilocks can't stomach." I sized her up, a small spark of curiosity burning at the thought.

Everyone knew on occasion The Agora would facilitate matters that were not morally sound as they liked to call it. They were neutral in all things at the core. It was a rule the Host insisted on. Maybe working for the goodie two shoes would mean I could meet the elusive one. Hell, if Death could come out of hiding, why not him.

"How does all that work anyway, Bloodsucker?"

"Jobs for The Agora equal payment or credit toward services. As a favor to me, Carissa is having a space set up for you in the same building as me. In truth, the same floor so I can keep an eye on you."

"Awe, we gonna have sleepovers too and braid each other's hair? Maybe I can come over and borrow a cup of sugar." I taunted.

"Look, I detest you as much as you detest me. However, something in my gut tells me not to kill you. Don't make me change my mind. Your life was forfeit to me. So, until I say otherwise, you're my bitch. When I say heel, you fucking heel. When I say jump, you fucking jump. And when I say behave, you shut that cock sucking hole of yours and do as you're told. Are we clear?" Jenna looked me in the eyes daring me to argue.

"Yes, ma'am. Though I do have one question." I paused till she nodded, "You gonna spank me if I misbehave?"

Her eyes lit to a blinding white forcing me to shut mine and shield them with my hands. Opening them when the light faded found her gone and my vision temporarily filled with spots.

"Fucking Hell." I muttered.

Jenna Devereaux once more proved that she was a force not to be toyed with. Unfortunately for her, I do so enjoy my games.

CHAPTER 21

~ MARCUS ~

Word reached me weeks ago. First as a rumor, then as fact. The Angel of Death had reemerged from a long slumber or hideaway. Many bore witness to his appearance at The Agora. His presence said to overwhelm all even with the dampening effects of the Host. The reports spoke of a female who had slapped him shortly after he arrived. I didn't need the full description to know the identity of the woman in question.

"Jenna. Jenna. Jenna. What have you gotten yourself into?" I spoke to the fire burning brightly.

Not sure why the fireplace was lit when the temperature was quite warm outside, but the witch seemed to always have one going whenever I stopped by. On the shelves were bottles, all pristinely labeled, baskets of what I wasn't certain, and dried herbs hanging along the edges. Anyone walking in would not think witch but perhaps someone who was into home remedies. The new craze going around no doubt delighted many who dabbled as ingredients were readily available.

What was done with those ingredients is where the differences began. Knowing how to channel the energy around us to conjure the desired result is what made a witch powerful. The more in touch with the energy, the stronger they were. Not merely witches but warlocks too. Some had a specialty they were gifted in while others were able to work in more areas. Very few could harness the power to do any kind of magic they wished without repercussions.

"I haven't heard you speak that name in a while. You missing your ward?" Constance questioned from the table.

"You know I don't do attachments. I simply heard the news about Death's return and the welcome she gave him at The Agora." I confessed.

"You know it isn't wise to lie to a witch, right?" she replied.

Did I miss Jenna? Sometimes. I would never admit to it though. She had become a very fond memory. One I drifted to when I let my mind wander. A time would come when our paths would cross again. Immortality would see to it. In truth, I had even purposefully been in her vicinity now and then. Catching a glimpse of her. Her dark brown hair catching the light of the sun. The way she would glance around as if she could sense me.

My breath had caught once when I thought I had been discovered only to have a Lycan jump out at her. Foolish creature actually seemed confident in its attack. One blow was all it landed. Her scent filled the air causing my fangs to elongate. I still craved her taste. What I told her before about how I would never forget it was true. When she tore the Lycan's head from his body and called in for clean-up, I waited. A junkie so close to another fix, I dashed out and sucked on the scrap of fabric, stained red, which had torn off during the abysmal fight. It beckoned me from where it lay on top of the deceased.

Even now I wonder what her blood may be capable of. Who could blame me when the word was spreading fast of her lineage? So many questions were answered. My demonic nature relished death. To snuff out the source of another with finality. Jenna was irresistible for that one simple fact. Her attitude, her independence, her intellect, those were mere bonuses. She presented a challenge at every turn. Even as one of our world, she would not let go of her morality when it came to what she classified as innocents.

"You're drifting again, Marcus. Do you want to come back after you have removed your dick from your shoulders?" The witch was getting impatient.

"Since when do you concern yourself with my dick? Wouldn't Genevieve get jealous?" I arched a brow at her.

I was aware that many witches were experiencing varying levels of frustration over the last few days. Their connections to the essence around us all was on the fritz. None of them seemed able to confirm why they were all having difficulties. As a result, there was to be a large meeting in a few days to discuss the investigation and possible solutions.

Not one to really use magic myself, I employed many who did. Their inability to provide was affecting my operations. Hence my appearance on Constance's doorstep. We went back centuries, and she looked exactly as she did when I met her. Ebony hair cascading down over ebony skin. A few strands fell over her shoulders lightly grazing the tops of firm breasts. She was a natural beauty with full curves that begged to be explored. For the last hundred years, only Genevieve has had that privilege.

"Can't you just pay someone off? Do you really need to have a presence at this meeting?" She sighed.

"They will discuss every possibility and reject anything they deem too dangerous or reckless. I will need the exact details of each plan if I am to decide how far I am willing to go to fix the problem. It's funny, would have thought you would be more on board with this." I stated as I ran a strand of her hair through my fingers.

Magic has kept her young but if the bond is severed, she will age quickly. One moment she could be here, the next moment her clothing could hold nothing but dust.

"You will need to catch a reaper. Their energy will be needed to complete the tonic. Just force them to drink it and they will be under your control. Reapers are known to wander everywhere. They won't raise suspicion when found hanging around the vicinity where almost all are cheating Death. While they remain, you can see and hear everything they do. But be warned, Death sometimes looks out for the reapers. At least that was the story when he was a memory." She poured the orange, fluorescent liquid into a bottle, dropping it in my hand as she finished.

"Not a problem. Trust me." I gave her one of my best smiles before vanishing back to my current residence.

Holding up the bottle, I twirled it in my hands while thinking of how this could change things. If only my witches and warlocks could touch the essence, there would be numerous things I could do without fear of repercussions. So many rules I could break simply for the fun of it.

"Perchance I would even visit Jenna. See if there is yet longing in her eyes." My smile grew at the mere notion.

CHAPTER 22

~ VANESSA ~

So much was different than I expected. I watched the world, the lives of those whose strings were cut, but still experiencing this for myself was a touch overwhelming. With focus, I could hide the strings of almost everyone. Those with strong destinies faintly glowed despite my best efforts. Luckily, there were only a few of them.

Jenna was of course one, Ademia was another, yet I dare not let her know, Carissa, the McKenzie brothers, and one that crossed through but had not fallen into place was another. Death or Salazar or Jack as Jenna likes to call him is the last one. His is more of a void though. A dark line cutting through all I see.

Fear over his frustration refuses to leave me. I am not sure any would survive if he decided he was done with everything. He says he loves Eve, what I have seen says he speaks the truth. Jenna refers to his affections as an obsession. One he needs to "get the fuck over" as she says. She is drawn to him. A fact she does not seem to like. I know she also believes he only loves who she was and not the woman she is.

Jenna was right at first. As he watched her, he first compared all to Eve. In time that faded, and he fell in love with her all over again for Jenna. Now, all our lives rest in her hands. Well, both their hands. The scales are tipping drastically with all being revealed.

Yesterday I sat with Alexander to avoid the demon. He was assisting a young witch with a basic spell, one to reveal a person's true nature. Five times he tried and five times he failed. It wasn't the first time I heard of issues connecting to the essence around us. Walking the halls of The Agora, many were grumbling about how their connections were failing.

Even those who did not use magic were experiencing waves of issues. Werewolves were having problems transforming both to and from their wolf forms. Some were now attempting not to turn for fear of not being able to come back.

Lycans reported aggressive outbursts from many in their packs. The anger rising for no apparent reason. Fatalities were unavoidable on many occasions. Vampires were not immune to the fluctuation either. More Rippers emerged while no new vampires could be sired.

The list went on and on. From fairies to nymphs to ogres and mermaids. Every species turned to their elders while their elders were turning to each other and The Agora. Over the next few days almost everyone would be there for a meeting to decide what to do.

"Kill them both or trap them in time." That will be the desire among most I thought out loud.

"Who are you killing?" Carissa asked, having just entered the library.

I turned to look at her. The sun filtering in through a

window made her hair appear to glow. In her yellow flowy dress, she seemed surreal. Carissa was almost always put together; I believe that's the right expression. Even on days when she wore jeans and a T-shirt, she radiated an energy that said she was ready for anything. However, she could not see it. Instead, she doubted herself frequently.

"No one. I was simply thinking aloud of the coming days." I confessed.

"And the coming days require a death or internment?" She questioned.

"They may. Fate has a plan, but the choices made by all keep it from settling. Fate pushes, or influences, strongly so in most." I stated.

"So, the stronger the will, the more freedom one has to shape their path. Make their own choices presented to them by fate." Carissa confirmed.

I didn't reply. The look on her face told me she was speaking for her own peace of mind then. Mortals and immortals alike did not accept being out of control when it came to their lives. They liked to blame fate, destiny, or luck when things went wrong instead of taking responsibility, yet anything good was *deserved* or earned.

"How are you settling in to being here, Vanessa?" Carissa broke the momentary silence.

"I have not felt them resurrect so I am fine with staying. When they return, so shall I." I responded.

"What if they never return? With everything happening, is it possible?" She turned to study me as she asked.

"I suppose anything is now." I confirmed.

The thought of returning to live alone for eternity caused a funny feeling in my chest. I missed my sisters and wanted them back. They were my world for as long as I could remember. The sun, moon, and stars we used to tease. We never settled on who was who. When they are reborn, maybe we can settle it. Maybe when they return, we will fall right back into our old ways. Till then, this void I feel won't ease. Every time I sense something, my heart races in anticipation of one being born.

I do feel for the parents though. When a Fate is born, we remain only a week before vanishing from their lives. Cruel? Yes. The time needed for us to connect to all around before assuming our role leaves us in their care. Once we leave them, we appear in our home already grown. From infant to woman in 7 days' time. At least we never had to suffer through puberty. I silently laughed to myself.

Carissa placed her hand on my shoulder, a gentle squeeze her only indication that she was leaving me to my thoughts. I smiled at her then glanced around to see so many perusing the stacks. All were seeking an answer to the chaos beginning to filter into their lives.

"If only the answers were available to you all." I whispered on a sigh.

The library appeared to go on forever. There were stacks all along the main floor with tables spotted here and there. A few fireplaces burned along the edges as well with comfortable chairs waiting for someone to enjoy some leisurely time. At regular intervals, stairs took one up a flight to access more books along the walls with a few cross sections of tables. That pattern repeated over and over again. Of course, one didn't have to climb the stairs if they didn't want to. There were elevators but not like those in the mortal world. Here, you stood in a circle on the floor, and you were simply taken to your destination. The circle was only a safety measure so people were not bumping into others. The library had many safety plans in place. One was the inability to burn or tear a page from a book.

None of the books could leave this space. Any attempt to do so only found the book back on its shelf. Would that magic still work? I believe it would. The Agora was the only place that had not experienced a problem. At least not that I was aware of. Those here still did though which was giving rise to rumors that the Host had something to do with it or had found a cure and was not sharing. Either way, it was building into trouble.

A few vampires conspired nearby, either ignorant or uncaring that I was seated here. They spoke of the meeting of the Elders and the demand they believed would be made. The Elders were going to require the Host attend. They wanted answers for all that was happening, and they wanted to make sure the Host was not hiding anything from them.

Chewing my lower lip, I left the library to go find Carissa or Joanna. They were kind to me, and I wanted to help them prepare. Passing rooms where witches, werewolves, Lycans, and fairies gathered I paused at each. Guilt made my skin flush from my chest to the tips of my ears but every time I heard the same demand, I felt more certain of my path.

Seeing a door off to my left, I quickly rushed over and knocked. A sense of relief washed over me at their voices ushing me in.

"Vanessa, how are you?" Joanna smiled.

"I am ok, but I have heard many of the clans, covens, dens, or whichever you call them speaking of their demands for the coming meetings. Each wishes to have the Host in attendance. Rather they all plan to demand so." I blurted out.

The two women looked at each other as if reading each other's thoughts. While they studied themselves, I studied them. Carissa was without a doubt, Joanna's daughter. The resemblance was unmistakable. Yet, I suddenly wondered where her father was. Was the Host Carissa's father?

I also noticed how the grey within Joanna's hair was spreading. As she took a less active role in managing The Agora, she was aging. She continued to command respect, and all listened to her, well except Jenna and even more so Ademia.

"Vanessa, I appreciate you bringing this to us. My mother and I will speak with the Host to see how they wish to proceed." Carissa's voice was soft but unmistakably firm.

"Good. As everything currently directly impacts me, I cannot see much to guide you further." I confessed.

"Your friendship and your support are more than enough." Carissa confided.

CHAPTER 23
~ SALAZAR ~

I sat in the in-between or purgatory as the mortals called it. This place has had many names: veil, weigh station, cosmic hold, place for lost souls, purgatory, judgment, where souls go when their life has been without any purpose to sway the scales. I shook my head in thought. Some of the references grew even more obscure while some remained rudimentary.

This place to me had become my safe haven. Surrounded by the reapers who were forced to pay penance and the souls that wandered. Death was everywhere in all its forms. The best part? No beings still living to grate my nerves. Since I first discovered Eve's essence, my mood improved while my mind set on one singular task.

The work needed to retrieve her energy, learn how to properly restore her, and remove a piece of myself was fraught with issues at every turn. Even now, hundreds of years later, I am left with questions I fear will have long lasting repercussions.

Another never-ending consequence of my actions is to keep her safe now that she has returned.

Eve's essence had been locked away by a witch in the depths of Hell. She existed so far inside a labyrinth of torture and grotesque creatures that nearly ten thousand souls perished trying to speak with her. The price she set for handing Eve over to me was the first to tip the scales. Her freedom which was never supposed to be had in exchange for that which I could not exist without. I can recall when I ventured to her to complete the deal.

The labyrinth was formed from cold, wet stone. Strange iridescent moss grew along the base, reaching up in equally unnerving patterns. Some reminded me of old runes, while others appeared to bear witness to my path. From the souls that had perished, I was able to get what I believed to be most of the maze mapped out.

Arrogance over being able to make my way through the rest carried me on. When my map ceased being useful, I dropped it on the ground to find the moss immediately consume the new addition. Bending over to examine it closer, what I bore witness to turned even my stomach. The moss was not moss at all. Instead, the combination of energies, souls as some believed, were forever bound here. This was the result of those already dead trying to reach the witch.

The rumor of the witch who could restore life or change fate began to spread amongst all. The living and the dead sought her out in desperate attempts at a second chance. From my research, none succeeded.

Turning a corner, spikes jutted out instantly from the wall on both sides. No trigger on the ground had been set, magic was at play here. Having walked cautiously, a single spike lanced through the back of my left shoulder. The tip barely poked through the front of my shirt though I felt the gaping wound when I pulled myself free.

My body began healing the moment the obtrusive object was gone. As the wound stitched closed, the spikes retreated back into the walls. Walking forward, curiosity reared. Was there anything here that could cause permanent damage or even kill me? Regardless of the answer, Eve was worth the risk.

The further in I went, the tighter the passage became. I considered unfurling my wings to fly over the towering walls but there was scarcely enough room for me to stand let alone attempt flight. Cheating certainly would have consequences as well.

I did have to turn back a couple of times, each causing my frustration to rise with my determination. I had to be close. Eve needed to be returned to me. If she was not, then all would pay for stealing her. Starting with this damn witch.

As the thought cemented itself in my mind, the center of the labyrinth appeared before me. Not the landscape of Hell that any imagined. Here, a small cottage sat surrounded by lush grass. A pond with a wooden bench sat off to the right, while a garden occupied the space to the left. Fireflies flitted about causing me to realize that the sky, or illusion thereof, was of the night. A full moon with bright stars filled where no doubt stone truly existed.

"You are late." A sultry voice beckoned.

"Excuse me." I scanned the grounds looking for the witch.

"I expected you about a decade ago." She replied as she stepped from behind a tree.

"I take it then that you know why I am here. Are you willing to give her to me?" I walked near to look down at the woman.

She had ebony hair with streaks of grey. Her skin was slightly tan, young, with silver eyeshadow framing almond shape eyes. Her black nails were filed to a point but were not the long talons I knew other witches to prefer. The gown she wore was black yet caught the moonlight to shimmer as she walked. The small sleeves hung loosely off her shoulders and I found my eyes lingering trying to recall the term for them. Attached to the corset style bodice, the skirt hung to her ankles revealing bare feet.

"You expected an old, disheveled woman." She laughed.

"I did. After hearing how long you have been imprisoned along with the power you are said to wield." I confessed.

"Sorry to disappoint. Though you bring up the very cost of winning your prize. I have been here too long. I desire only my freedom in exchange for the essence you seek." She stopped to sit on the bench.

"Do you know what it would take to free you?" I asked.

"Yes. I will have to absorb your dearly beloved as well as a piece of you. Your combined strength will allow me to leave here. Then, I will return both to you." She spoke while watching the fish I caught a glimpse of in the pond.

"How the fuck am I supposed to trust you?" My eyes morphed into a swirl of black and white.

"You cannot judge me. Also, you don't have a choice. When I felt you near, I already took her in. So, all I need now is you. Now choose or accept that she is lost to you forever." Her voice at last hinted at the power she held as everything shook around us.

"For her I will do anything. Double cross me and I will end you in the vilest way I can imagine." I confirmed.

She rose with a smile on her lips. When near, she stood on her tip toes, laced her fingers behind my neck and kissed me. The moment our lips touched I felt her draining me. For the first time in my entire existence, I was weakened physically. Closing my eyes, I opened them again to find us standing in a corn field.

"Where are..." I didn't get to finish my question.

A shot of light burst from her, my strength slamming back into my body along with the addition of the mortal essence I longed for. When the light faded, the witch stood there staring up at the moon.

"Right on time to start setting things in motion." She whispered.

"What is your name, witch? What are you planning to do now?" A chill ran down my spine as I studied her.

"I will not be causing harm to you or your precious *Missing Piece*. Do not fret. You will not even hear of me for a *very* long time." She began to walk away.

"Your name?" I called out.

"Luna." She said softly before vanishing.

She was honest at least. I have not heard of her causing any trouble or doing anything at all. Not sure if that should worry me more or not. At the end of the day, I didn't really care. She had given me my Missing Piece back.

CHAPTER 24

~ JENNA ~

After Carissa left, I stood at the floor to ceiling windows in my bedroom. Outside the sky let loose a downpour already causing puddles on the road below. People scurried from one place to another in a futile attempt to avoid being drenched.

There was a small ledge just on the other side. Without thought, I opened the large window to step up on the table and escape into the thundering call of the city. In an instant, the cold barrage soaked every inch of my body. My head arched up, frustration that had been building for weeks demanded release in the camouflage. Surrendering, silent tears left my eyes to disappear in the droplets making streams down my cheeks.

Lightning crashed above, the loud boom rattling the glass behind me. I needed the chaos of the storm to challenge the torment within. Another streak lit the sky followed by another striking the building across from where I stood.

As the clouds screamed, they vanished. Searching my new reality found a field. Somewhat overgrown, a tree standing tall in the middle of a clearing with a stream not far off. Familiarity had me feeling sad, peaceful, excited, and furious.

"Where are you?" I called out.

Stepping from behind the cherry tree, he strode over to me. When near enough, I slapped him hard. The sound echoed around us.

"You really must stop that." He spoke without moving.

"Fuck you. Why the fuck did you bring me here?" I demanded.

"I thought you might enjoy it. Need it even given all that has happened. This was always a place of peace for you, for Eve." Salazar confessed.

"I am not her. How many times do I have to tell you? I have her memories and I will admit I feel drawn to you. A connection I can't explain, and I don't fucking like it."

"Jenna, I don't expect you to be her or be different. Who you are is the person you were meant to be. A woman I adore, my Missing Piece always. I know you don't believe it or me. You will though." He spoke so confidently.

"Like Hell." I spat out wishing words could cut.

He grabbed my arm dragging me to the tree. For the first time since I began training, I could not free myself. Slamming my back against the tree, he pushed till I sat in the small split of branches. Motioning to stand when he let go, he raised a brow daring me to flee. Sitting back down I watched him pluck a cherry off a branch and twirl it in his fingers.

"You need time to relax, get your bearings." Salazar calmly explained.

"How the fuck do you know what I need? Hell, don't pretend like you care anyway. All you care about is getting your precious Piece back." I hated how I sounded like a toddler on the verge of a tantrum or a jealous teenager ready to listen to a mixed tape.

"YOU ARE MINE." His composure fractured, I studied how his eyes swirled with black and white.

"Except you were wrong already about one thing. My wings aren't the inky black color of yours but a pure white that almost seem to glow." I arched a brow.

"Interesting." He responded.

He stepped closer, the knuckle of his index finger pressing under my chin till I looked deep into his eyes. All the emotions I denied swelled the longer we were locked together. I hated feeling this way when I wasn't sure I had a choice in the matter. What was this? Obsession? Infatuation? Curiosity? Lust? Love?

My mind lost the thread it was set on tugging when his hand clamped down on the back of my neck. His lips found mine, my hands pressed against his chest without forcing him away. Instead, my hands fisted in his shirt, nails elongating in vampiric delight.

"I hate you." I managed to squeeze out between the magnetic attraction of our lips.

"I hate you so much. I hate you for what you have done to me. To my life. For not protecting me if I was so precious to you. You left me to him, his will. Why didn't you save me from him? Why didn't you stop Victor? Why didn't you save Eve? Take her away from Adam?" Tears streamed down my face, some finding their freedom in their descent while others were swallowed between us.

Our hands tore our clothing from our bodies. Heat rose between us as our nails scored our flesh. The aroma filled the air, faint from the healing wounds, as it mixed with the scent of the forest surrounding us. Sun filtered through the leaves above, casting shadows that danced around us.

I despised myself for this need. He was an instant addiction, desire to have him near, to touch him, to be enveloped in his scent, to feel his arms around me. He felt like home, safe, familiar, all the while conjuring a rising ire for the disappointment in his choices.

How could I want someone so much it bordered on need? Fighting this pull only seemed to make the energy between us explode. I didn't care. He didn't deserve me and I couldn't trust him. He has proven he will do anything to get what he wants regardless of what it means for others.

"Stop thinking." He groaned.

"Bastard. You are the epitome of a bastard." I gasped, his hands sliding down my body to stroke the bare lips of my cunt.

"I have to taste you, Jenna." His voice was a breathy whisper against my neck.

Prepared for him to bite me, he kissed my skin instead. A trail cut down my body, stopping to suck on my nipples, his hands massaged each possessively. My head fell back against the rough bark, my right hand fisting in his hair the lower he dropped. On his knees, he wrapped each arm under my legs to lift me up and place each thigh on his shoulders.

He placed a slow kiss, sucking on the top of my clit before working his way lower to plunge his tongue into my depths. My back arched, nails scraping his scalp the tighter my body became.

"Fuck!" I cut out when I felt his tongue begin to move faster.

He sucked, licked, and fucked my core, my muscles grew taught with the need to let go. Without warning, his wings erupted from his back, teeth grazed my skin, and I lost my control. Sweat beginning to bead along my flesh, I cried out only to have him swallow my voice with his lips.

His eyes were swirling black and white, realization dawning

that my own were a mix of color as well. Red lining the black and white, the only difference in our gazes. My fangs elongated to match the longer set smirking back at me. Surprised, I returned his grin a second before he claimed my mouth. Hearing wood crack from behind, he drove forward filling me. Another sensation of belonging, of being right washed over me. I pushed the notion aside, reminding myself of all he had done. All he had permitted to be done allegedly on my behalf.

Anger fueled white wings rushed forward sending us both to the ground. With him on his back, my blackened nails tore down his chest. Leaning over to lick up the crimson trail, the power I tasted sent my hips riding harder against him. Using him, his body, his desire, to release the tension coursing through mine was what I needed.

Everything from the moment I met Victor to the last 10 minutes flowed into my actions. Hot tears released of their own accord; a glow began to radiate around us. Bright. Warm. Humming with energy.

My mind tried to break in, alerting me to the change in our environment but I did not care nor did he. At least he did not react. Emotions ruled, need to forget the dominant force. Everything was poured into the here and now. Tomorrow did not exist, hell anything after this did not exist. There was only his body and mine.

Possessing kisses, teeth occasionally nicking lips to release droplets of blood, hands, nails dragging down flesh, the sound of skin pounding into another, nothing else mattered. Sitting up, he held onto my shoulders from around my back, his hips driving up to meet mine. Harder, faster, he gripped tighter to take control. On my back, my wings rose on either side to shield us from the world.

"You can hate me, despise me, wish the ground would

swallow me, but I will always be yours." He punctuated every word with a thrust of his hips.

Claiming my mouth, he drove forward as we both fell apart. He laid his head on mine, pleading in his eyes to prolong the moment. Part of me wanted to give in. I couldn't. My past. My present. My future would not let me.

Shoving him off, I grabbed my clothes, dressing quickly before turning on him.

"Take me home. Now." I said.

"Jenna..." He began.

"Now, Jack." I raised a brow, making certain to use his nickname.

Such a powerful being standing in front of me looking like someone just clipped his wings did nothing to change my mind. I could not let anyone ever control me again.

CHAPTER 25
~ SALAZAR ~

She was done with me for now. I had the need to see her, talk to her yet I had not anticipated where my visit would lead. I definitely was not complaining, Her taste still lingered on my tongue, bringing a slight smile to my lips.

Risking further upsetting her, I did not take her home. Taking us both to the garden at The Agora, I walked near the water, studying the fountain.

"We were happy. She was my Missing Piece. To be honest, I wasn't sure bringing her energy back would feel even a fraction of what it had." I confessed.

"And does it?" She asked, shaking her head as soon as the words were free.

"No." I watched her shoulders slump ever so slightly, "You are not Eve. Yet, you have her same independence in you. Eve was not as decisive, nor was she as guarded. I know you have suffered a lot and you survived it all to become stronger. Your confidence, your acceptance of this world, your place in it. I don't love you because you are her. I am yours, Jenna, because of who you are."

She kept her distance from me, not saying a word. Giving her time to absorb my statement, I waited. Would she continue to fight what we mean to each other? She has Eve's memories and part of me within her. We once more sated our needs in each other. She feels for me, but is it because of the memories or because of my essence used to bring her to life? Her energy was so powerful, my energy was needed to stabilize it.

Cutting my eyes back to the fountain, I watched a purple salamander travel up my stone reflection to perch on the cold shoulder. The creature faced me as if sizing me up. About to eliminate the tiny thing, Jenna appeared beside me lowering my hand.

"Don't even think about it." She stated coldly.

Here was an example of something I would have to work on or else she may never accept me. She truly did not wish for any animal, human or otherwise to suffer. Her only exception being spiders. For some reason, she detested them. Actually, most insects were not given a second thought. Dragonflies were an exception to this as were butterflies and bees.

That she held any compassion only made me care for her more. She was tough and soft, smart and yet still had so much to learn, and lethal. The last part was something I would have to help her with. No one else could. It was my original purpose for calling on her.

"When would you like to discuss what you are and all you can do as Death? There are aspects you should learn to control to keep those around you safe." Playing on her caring for others, the anticipation of getting to spend more time with her made me feel a strange sensation in the pit of my stomach.

"I have had enough fucking training and I haven't hurt anyone I didn't damn well intend to ever since." She scolded.

"Ok then. Do you know why taking someone's life is not the first thing I do in a fight? The cost or weakness that results? Have you yet touched someone so deeply they can see all their horrors or their blessings? There are skills I can teach you that no one else can. Only I know what I am capable of. However, no one knows the extent transferred over to you." I cupped her cheek, taking advantage of her intense gaze.

When she realized I was touching her, she pulled back as if burned. We had just spent a couple hours fucking and now she acted as if my touch repulsed her. Perhaps because deep down it didn't is why she reacted in such a way.

"I've figured out a lot on my own, why the fuck do I need you? You're no Mr. Miyagi after all." She quipped.

"I wouldn't need chopsticks to catch a fly and I sure as hell would not tolerate anyone bullying you. They would all die the moment they touched you. If I had not worried over frightening you, Marcus would have died long ago." I confirmed.

"That pleasure will be mine if he ever dares to show his wretched face again. He is not the man I had hoped he would be." She spoke with conviction, but I swore I saw melancholy in her gaze.

She opened her mouth to say more but we were interrupted by Carissa, Vanessa, and Ademia. I knew each well from the tabs I had kept on my Missing Piece. Carissa had her hair in a ponytail with a few strands falling around her face. Her sage tank top was tucked into her tan pants that hugged her body down to her brown boots. Clean, authoritative, and so in contrast with the black-haired demon beside her. Ademia was in a single black tank that was loose with a couple tears daring a malfunction to occur, her red bra straps showed as a black strap of her shirt fell down her arm. Her matching torn black pants ended in spiked black boots that did not attempt to hide a small dagger at each side. Vanessa seemed so out of place between the two. Her red hair and pale skin washed out further in her pale sundress that almost touched the floor. She walked barefoot with a smile on her face as if on a casual stroll. It struck me how odd the three of them looked together, when one knew who they were.

"Hey Bloodsucker, who's the hottie?" Ademia greeted us.

"Fuck off, *Addy*. I have no time for your bullshit." Jenna replied.

Ademia glared at the nickname but did nothing to retaliate. Vanessa hid a small smile watching everyone interact while Carissa cleared her throat.

"We will get nowhere if you two start going after one another. Besides, you are both aware that it will do you no good. The Agora and your own bond will not permit any true harm to come to one another. The only exception being that Jenna can still forfeit your life, Ademia, as per the agreement in the duel." Carissa was calm, notes of exhaustion coloring her words.

"We should speak somewhere more private." I interjected.

"That would be wise. There are already others listening." Vanessa added.

In an instant, we were in Carissa's office. Not something normally done if the confused expressions on the others' faces were any indication. Joanna stood in the corner with a scolding look directed at Carissa. Their energies were familiar, a smirk lining my lips at the sight.

"That explains a lot." I whispered.

CHAPTER 26
~ CARISSA ~

"We have four hours till the first delegates will arrive. The heads of every house, species, clan, coven, pack, den, and more will be in attendance. Every one of them will be asking for the cause of the rift and every one of them will want action taken against the two of you." I reminded them all.

"I am not hearing a problem here, Goldilocks." Ademia sat on the edge of the table closest to the window twirling a curved dagger in the air and catching it.

"If I die, my last act will be to bind you to The Agora for eternity. To live in a single room here and only be permitted out to do their bidding, Addy. You will be a good little servant." Jenna grinned.

"Can she fucking do that? Ain't it if she dies, I'm free?" Ademia questioned.

"She can and I do believe she would." I confirmed.

"Ladies, I can assure you all that it will not come to that. No one will harm her." Salazar interjected.

"Awe, aren't you just a damn white knight clad in black and reeking of sex. Yeah, I can smell the sin on both of ya." Ademia mocked, pointing her dagger at Salazar and Jenna.

Salazar simply spread his black wings, his eyes swirling an inky black mixed with a glowing white. His skin became ashen the longer he stood then began to darken to match the clothes he wore. All of us stood transfixed by what we were witnessing. Gone for so long from the world, no one knew what was fact or fiction where he was concerned. Standing here now, I could confirm that when he wanted to, he could emit a bone deep coldness which would not be ignored.

"Enough. Both of you put your dicks away." Jenna walked casually to the bar.

"I just wanted to push his buttons a little. Tempt Death." Ademia chuckled.

"Grow up, Addy." Jenna replied in a bored tone.

"All of you need to listen. Jenna and Salazar will be in attendance though you will not have formal seating. I ask that you do not interfere unless absolutely necessary. We will attempt to discuss the cause of the issue without naming either of you. Doing so will, without a doubt, derail the entire purpose of the meeting." My tone held the authority I struggled with when addressing them.

"And what am I s'posed to do?" Ademia spoke up, fire lighting her eyes.

"Sit in your room with Vanessa like a good little demon." Jenna answered.

"We cannot have them see the Fate so you will guard her." I clarified.

"You mean babysit." Ademia snarled.

"Yes." Salazar responded, a smirk playing on his lips.

"What the fuck ever. At least I can play with my Trinket." Ademia laughed.

I permitted a door to appear, pointing to it without a word. Ademia took the hint, grabbing Vannessa's hand to drag her along on her way out and leaving us to speak more freely. The Fate was of no use to us now anyway as the events were too closely entwined with her own path.

"Ok, now that they're gone. What the fuck aren't you telling us, Carissa?" Jenna demanded.

I took a deep breath, they needed to be prepared but really, I wondered if any of us truly could be. Glancing at my mother, who shook her head no while trying to speak to me through our link, I hoped she saw in my gaze why I felt this was the right thing to do.

"We may need their help, mother. There has never been a crisis like this and keeping our secret is no longer something I believe we can do alone." I pleaded, my gaze surveying the room.

Jenna looked on expectantly while Salazar crossed his arms. My mother stepped forward to stop me but it was Salazar who put an end to it all. With three little words, our secret was out.

"You are Gods." Salazar stated.

I nodded solemnly, my mother casting her eyes down to the floor. There are all types, manner of our kind, and a reason we hide our identity from all. For us, there was an even greater reason.

"We are." I confirmed.

"Well don't expect me to bow down and kiss your feet or pray to you. Fucking hell! You need some kind of damn sacrifice before you step the fuck up and fix this shit?" Jenna exclaimed.

"Jenna, it's not like that. Gods are not as all powerful as some think. We don't even call ourselves that. We call ourselves Celestials because we are of the very energy of the universe. As such, we can manipulate elements or things. We were worshipped long ago. However, some discovered how to imprison us, make us do their bidding or link with us to make themselves stronger. Others found a way to absorb us entirely. For us specifically, we are punished due to the actions of my father. He sought to end the conflict and interfered with a pact being made. None of us knew the full extent of the agreement." I tried to keep my emotions in check but tears found their release anyway.

"The Host. It's your father. But I've met multiple generations of your family." Jenna said.

"I apologize for the deception. It's another trick of The Agora. Others see us age, see us as a child who grows, but really, we are always us. The memory I had of my mother and me as a baby happened so long ago. Even my memory of me playing in the garden of The Agora was not long after my father's judgement was passed. The Agora is actually like the home we had lived in. As my father had liked to interfere, he was cast with never being able to again. The curse froze him in time. That is why none can harm each other here. If there is no real time passing, others are frozen to a degree. That and they are not permitted to cut another's life short as what became of that pact. Two had died that day because of his actions. We can leave The Agora, in doing so we look as we are which is as we look now. Celestials age extremely slowly." I explained.

"Ok, let me see if I have this straight. You're Celestials; your father is here somewhere frozen in time; and you can't break the curse of your punishment. Also, others would love to get their hands on you to make you their bitch or have you for dinner? That about sum this shit up?" Jenna summarized.

"Yes." Joanna spoke.

"Why don't you seem surprised or anything really?" Jenna asked Salazar.

"Taking a close look at them, I knew what they were. It also explained why when you were in their presence, my connection to you was weak." Salazar replied.

"You really are a jackass, Jack." Jenna stated and despite myself, I found myself laughing.

The tension cut, we all agreed to protect our secret and help dissuade the elders of all those attending from demanding the Host show himself. After all these years, it felt really good to have that weight lifted from my shoulders. To be able to really just be me.

CHAPTER 27
~ MARCUS ~

"Fucking hell!" I screamed, my hands wrapping around the woman's throat.

She was an innocent. Her brown eyes reminding me of Jenna, which made the same familiar nugget of something I refused to name creep up. This woman needed to die if I was going to bring a reaper forth. I had no idea if it was her time or not, nor did I really care. All that mattered was getting eyes and ears into that meeting. I purposefully waited till the time was drawing near so Death couldn't have a chance to sense the change in the damn thing.

I despised feeling this way. Ever since Jenna left, the look of disappointment and disgust left this strange sensation in its wake. Some days, I almost hated her for it. Thoughts of perhaps killing her to rid myself of this flitted through my mind now and then. Not foolish enough to try, instead I hoped to one day have her look at me differently. Then the damned thing might go away. That, and I would have her back. I even made another deal to help with returning her to me and ridding us of the obstacle I saw standing in the way.

"What did you do to me?" I asked, the woman's eyes growing more frantic.

She knew she was going to die. Her final plea was not to harm her little girl in the next room. I think fear of waking her is what finally silenced her screams before I even crushed her windpipe. Now she was hanging on by a thread. The light in her eyes grew dim until no sign of life shown in their depths.

The room became colder, a smile growing across my face. One of them was coming to collect her soul. It was then that I realized I was still grasping her throat in my hand. Letting go, she dropped to the floor in a heap. Her sacrifice might allow me to help those I employed reconnect with their energies. Even if no others could, hell it would be better for me if they couldn't. A monopoly on the connection would be very good for business.

"Right on time." I said just as the Reaper materialized.

Quickly, I did as instructed to finish the spell before the damned soul could retreat or signal for assistance. Part of me wanted to see Death. Face him for sending Jenna my way and for then taking her from me. I had learned how the church always found us. Messages from the one and only. Of course, once she was on their radar, it wasn't their only means of tracking her movements.

Refocusing on the task at hand, I stared into the Reapers' eyes thankful for my demonic essence. As a mere vampire, I would not have been able to clearly see or touch the wretched thing. He looked to be about 50, greying hair, portly figure, with an outfit that screamed corporate lacky. His suit was nice enough but not fitted and not a name brand. His tie hung loosely around his neck with the top button undone as well.

Looking him over, I would guess heart attack while sitting at his desk trying to meet some deadline he thought was so important.

"You will do as I command. Attend the meeting at The Agora. Do not draw attention to yourself but remain there until the meeting is over." I whispered so as not to wake the child.

The Reaper faded into nothing with a nod. He would do as he was told since he didn't really have a choice in the matter. Those assholes will be clueless. Serves them right as none have the balls to do what it takes to fix this mess anyway.

One by one they began filling the large circular room. I couldn't help but be reminded of the room I'd seen on tv during the political interruptions I ignored. Here the incline was much steeper to allow all to see one another. The stone walls rose up and seemed to disappear into a white ceiling. Each being having their own chair or chairs which I assumed they chose. They were in sections as well. Vampires. Werewolves. Lycans. Fairies. Mermaids. Kelpies. Witches. Demons. Angels. Ogres. Trolls. Elves. Nymphs. Sirens. The list went on and on.

Part of me chuckled inwardly that we were only missing a damn unicorn and old Nessie, the Loch Ness Monster. A chill ran up my spine, momentarily halting my amusement. A reaper floated through the space, visible yet seemingly without physical form. The man, dressed in slightly disheveled suit, wandered around passing through those seated. Each shivered in turn when contact was made. Even the vampires were not spared the sensation.

In the center, Carissa sat on a large wooden bench that curved up on each side allowing her to rest her arms. Joanna sat on a smaller version to her right while a matching one sat empty on the left. She looked like a Queen missing her royal attire and crown. Hell, even her posture was straight as a board.

When everyone was seated, Carissa spoke gently, her voice carrying easily to all. I stood in the back of the room leaning against the wall. I had forbidden Ademia and Vanessa from attending. Something told me that would make all this a thousand times worse.

"I wish to thank you all for attending. The current crisis has grown to such lengths it requires us all to work together." Carissa greeted.

"Then why is the Host not here? If this is so dire, where is he?" A frail, older woman's voice called out.

Carissa's eyes turned to meet the fairy, the twitch I noted in her muscles the only sign of her unease.

"He is unable to attend. As you all know, he is completely aware, and I will speak on his behalf. This is how it has always been done and how it will remain." Carissa responded.

Grumbling started up. Quiet at first, the sound began to grow more intense. I could sense the outrage, the fear, and the hatred over being kept at a distance. Sensing where this was heading, I leapt down to stand in front of Carissa and Joanna. Knowing their secret now, I felt the need to protect them even more.

"You are all a bunch of fucking children. Why can't we see him? Why does he only speak to you? Why am I not special? My damn feelings are hurt, and I need a nappy." I paused to look around the room.

"For fuck's sake. Look, the connection for everyone to whatever makes everyone what they are is on the fritz. We have all hit the side of the tv, sprayed our WD-40, and gotten out our duct tape but it's still broken. Now we can continue sitting around with our thumbs up each other's asses or we can work together for a solution." I concluded while watching some look down like a scolded toddler, others looked like they wanted my head for daring to speak to them that way.

"We need to know how this happened in order to figure out how to fix it." A witch spoke, her long ebony hair flowing down to her hip and bright green eyes matching her dress focused on me.

Well, fuck me. I groaned. We all knew this was inevitable. Carissa was hesitant about me attending for this very reason. Before I could open my mouth to admit my very existence was the cause she sought, Salazar appeared beside me.

"This is the result of my doing. There was something I had to get back. So much so that if I did not, I was going to destroy all of you and everything." He stated flatly to keep with Carissa's warning of not revealing the depth of the reason. Us.

For several minutes no one spoke or moved or seemed to breathe. They all knew he was here. Those that hadn't heard the rumors before the meeting were quickly caught up by others when they arrived. The power emanating off of him confirmed he was real. Glancing up at him, I couldn't conjure the same fear or amazement. To me, he was and will always be 'Jack the jackass'.

"What did you need?" A strong male voice with a German accent shredded the quiet blanket. One look his way screamed Centaur.

My mind screamed for him not to answer, or not answer directly. Keep being vague enough. Listen to what Carissa said in the office. One word spoken crushed any chance of me not becoming public enemy number one.

"Her." He replied.

The uproar rising in response confirmed Carissa's fears. All were looking to one another then to us. Without thought, I found my hand reaching for his. When our fingers intertwined, I felt stronger.

"Quiet." Joanna's voice boomed and all ceased their speculations.

"What is done is done. Death is willing to help us all find a solution. As is Jenna. I know what some may be thinking, kill Jenna and the balance will be restored. However, we can assure you it won't work. Also, Death has given us his oath. If anyone harms her, he will kill all of us. Not just those in this room, but everyone." Carissa informed them.

I saw how they tried to size him up. Could he really do it? Would he really do it? Hell, I wondered the same thing too, but I wasn't willing to put it to the test. Were any of them? Fuck, could I even die? So far, I have been hurt severely a few times, but I've survived everything. Were any in this room capable of doing more? Did I really want to find out?

"What are our options then?" An ogre called out.

"Jenna and Death will have to set the scales right. The universe will assist with tasks to balance itself. Right now, the balance is off. We will need everyone to report any matters they might normally handle internally to The Agora. We will work through them to see if any could be related to tipping the scales. If they are, you must agree to let The Agora and Jenna or Death handle the matter." Carissa stated much calmer than I expected.

"You expect us to reveal all of our clans' affairs to you?" A Lycan spoke up with others grumbling their agreement.

"For the time being, it is the only way." Joanna replied first.

"We know what we ask is unprecedented and against all

traditions. We give you our word that the information will only be seen by the four of us. All replies will be swift as well, so we do not interrupt your ruling." I answered.

"How will you know which matters to attend?" An elder vampire questioned.

"The Host will show us the way." Carissa replied, yet I knew she was lying.

This was going to either be by Vanessa's guidance or by sheer luck. Yet, she was right, this was our best option to balance the scales. Letting go of his hand, I crossed my arms under my breasts. Slowly my eyes morphed from red to black to a blinding white then a mix of all three. I watched as many shielded themselves and others slunk down to hide. Beside me, I caught the glimpse of ebony wings and let my own free. They needed to see they really had no choice. It was then that I saw something else, apparently, I wasn't the only one.

The Reaper was there one moment then a fluttering mist of debris the next. I had sensed the aura of the passenger which made me feel sick yet relieved. Marcus was still alive but was up to his tricks. He had learned nothing over the years. Only confirming that one day, I would have to kill him.

To the others, it seemed a show of strength if the gasps were any indication. It worked. One by one, each acquiesced to the request. Coming down from their seats to discuss timing and transport of the information. Carissa handed a letter sized envelope to each. All they had to do was write down the situation and place it in the envelope. The information would be relayed directly here for our review. If it came back unmarked, it was not a scale related issue. Otherwise, a letter would arrive in its place of next steps.

I was slightly amused and annoyed how they treated

Carissa with disdain then acted as if he was a God. If they only knew. Then again, was dear Jack a Celestial too?

Back in Carissa's office, we sat in the chairs facing her desk. Jenna had poured herself a glass of bourbon before taking her seat. A chair she moved slightly away from mine. Carissa entered after us, taking her place behind the desk which sat bare save for a small stack of blank parchment, an oil well, and a single white quill. I knew within the drawer she kept a small laptop and a large monitor had been on her desk during my last visit to this room.

"Resorting to the old ways?" I broke the silence.

"Many of the leaders still prefer communication this way. I have the feeling I will be writing a lot in the coming days thanks to you." She replied.

Two upset females. How could one man be so fortunate? Why could they not understand that I was not about to lie? I was not ashamed of what I had done for I would do it again and again if necessary. I dare any to challenge me or hurt her. I would end them all. In doing so I would destroy myself. The cost would be worth the act.

"Jenna, you are unusually quiet. What are you thinking?" Carissa asked.

She didn't reply. Instead, her glass tipped the rest of the amber liquid down her throat. Her rage rolled off her in waves. Her aura was colored with it. Gone was the scent I caught earlier of her pheromones rising in my presence. She was on a different kind of edge. Needing to kill, hunt, or hurt something to release her ire. I did not like angering her. Pushing her away was never my intent when I only longed to have her near.

"You fucking asshole. Jackass doesn't even begin to cover what a monumental shitstorm you have conjured. Why? Why couldn't you just give them some half truth or lie for fuck's sake. Do you realize how much more complicated you made matters? Do you really think some of them won't try some shady bullshit to undermine Carissa and kill me? I will have to kill them instead. People I wouldn't normally have to kill. All because you don't give a shit, Jack." Jenna spoke, her voice never rising which made each word sound even more deadly.

She had been thinking of this since the meeting. Since I had revealed her link to me. We stood there for hours while everyone came to speak to Carissa before they departed. Hours without a word. Now I knew what she had been consumed with that entire time.

"You are incorrect. I care a great deal. Yet, the extent of my feelings start and end with you. I will assist in undoing the damage I have caused to ensure we can continue on. Other than that, I am yours to command." I held up a hand.

"Do not ask me to leave you though. That is the one thing I will not do." I felt something tickle from my back up my right shoulder.

Turning my head, a hint of purple caught my eye. The little salamander I had seen in the garden sat perched casually, his head facing me. I raised my hand to flick or incinerate the tiny creature. Deciding as my fingers prepared to act, only as I made my choice, a hand came down on my own. My gaze cut to meet Jenna's, disapproval in her own making me sigh.

"What now?" I groaned.

"You really have no respect for the life of anything else, do you? Well, if you want me to give you a chance, that has to change. We can start small with this little guy. Consider him your own personal Jiminy Cricket. Maybe he can turn you into a real boy." She arched a brow, daring me to deny her request.

"As you command, my Missing Piece." I replied softly.

"Good. You and uh, Jack Jr. will become good friends. I have no doubt about it." She smiled a little, the small gesture making my own lips curl.

"Are you two about done?" Carissa interjected, reminding us we were not alone.

"I apologize, Carissa. Lying is not something I really do, nor do I feel it necessary. The balance will be restored as I will not permit anything to jeopardize our future. As Jenna cares for others, so will I. Those in her inner circle shall be protected from now on." I placed my hand over my heart, demonstrating the depth of my oath.

"We will all be facing dangers in the coming days. I can feel the balance shifting, something darker is at work just out of sight." Vanessa spoke quietly as she entered the room.

"Sounds like a good time. Finally." Ademia followed right behind her.

"I am glad you feel that way, Addy. Seems the vampires have their hands full with some blood junkies. Many have gotten to the point of no return and began to change. I'm sure you will have no reservations about dispatching those beyond hope and imprisoning the others." Jenna informed.

"No problem at all. Rippers are known for being stronger since they are basically animals. Their unpredictability is always amusing too." Ademia grinned, fire dancing in her eyes.

"Great. One matter settled." Carissa stated.

Ademia turned to walk out the door, stopping when Jenna's voice rang out.

"Oh, and Addy dear. No torturing the ones to be saved."

Ademia snarled, whether at the command or nickname, I wasn't certain. Either way, she would have to obey. Kopis daggers at her hips, I noted the push daggers sticking out of the black boots she wore. The silver handle was unmistakable against the skin-tight black pants topped by a loose black tank top over a matching red one. Both shirts and her jeans had holes in them. I began to think about Jenna's previous assertion of wearing something other than black.

She gave Jenna a wink accompanied by a quick salute before opening the door. On the other side stood an alite group of vampire soldiers. No doubt their superiors already told them of our assistance. None appeared surprised nor pleased to see the demon step from the doorway. Behind them was the head-quarters for the east coast vampire elder. They had actually erected a doorway in the middle of a field with the agreement that The Agora only open to that door and never within their dwelling.

The green grass rose up to meet the large house we could see framed in the opening. It looked like a lovely place from the outside with an abundance of windows. Obviously, the majority of those in residence were immune to the effects of the sun.

As the door closed, we could hear Ademia greet the others, "Well hello boys. Who's ready for some mayhem?"

CHAPTER 30
~ CARISSA ~

One issue dealt with, a million more to go. Whether out of spite or actual compliance, many of the leaders had divulged issues within their ruling. The one on the east coast was the most dire as the risk of exposure was the greatest. The remaining tasks were all within reason as mundane. However, Vanessa would be the one to confirm our assessment.

Wearing a long, pale pink dress, I watched her. The thin straps were hidden by her red locks. As come to be expected, she was barefoot as well. She walked over to the table where we had set out all of the requests, her hand hovering over them as her eyes shimmered. Plucking one up, she held it to her chest with a sad expression.

"The rest are not weighty enough to assist with the balance. This one is special though." Her soft voice seemed to whisper.

"Ok, so we start with that one." Salazar agreed.

"No. Not yet. It's too soon." Vanessa held the paper tighter to her body.

"So, what are we supposed to do then?" Jenna asked.

"Train." I answered.

"I know Death, um, Salazar, said there is more you should learn. So, learn. We will need you both at your best, I fear." I continued.

"You are correct." Salazar confirmed.

"Fine." Jenna conceded.

"Jenna, he is telling you the truth. I cannot see the specifics. All I can confirm is your defeat without knowing all you are capable of as well as the consequences. There are reasons he doesn't go around killing everyone. Reasons your instincts have kept you from doing so in a fight as well." Vanessa's golden eyes showed genuine concern.

"Gees, I already agreed. Can we stop the fucking feeling factory?" Jenna shuddered.

I could tell she still had trouble with connecting. Alone for so long, then betrayed by Marcus. She even felt betrayed by Salazar. Our friendship did not even really click into natural until after the cave. I felt when she accepted our bond. Even when it deepened after revealing our secret to her.

There was more to share, at some point. She no doubt wanted to know what we are capable of. How many of us exist? Is there a way to tell who we are? How to kill our kind? Jenna would forever be on guard. Defensive. Desiring to be prepared for any battle. It was only her defiance at spending more time with him that kept her from already training.

"You will have full use of any services we can provide." I confirmed with a nod to Salazar.

"We won't need them. Your barriers will not be able to contain us at full strength. Jenna and I will need to return to my dwelling if she is to release her full power without causing harm to others." He replied.

"Only way to get a woman home, huh?" Jenna scoffed.

I could only shake my head while watching them all depart. Vanessa continued her secure hold of the file as she left with a small smile on her lips.

Alone in my office, I sealed myself in with a thought. I needed time alone. Something in short supply lately as mother took a step back. Closing my eyes, a yawn escaped freely, my head falling back against the chair.

My whole body felt heavy. Starting from my feet to travel up my legs, through my chest to the ends of my fingertips. Breathes becoming slower, I could feel as I drifted off. Surrendering to the allure of the dream world, I sighed.

A meadow with a pond in the center lay before me. To the right was a stone pathway leading to a white gazebo, a small lantern hanging in the center that dazzled in the fading light of day. As dusk ruled the scene, I glanced down to see the flowing black gown covering my body.

Feeling peaceful, I made my way in my bare feet up the steps to find two glasses of champagne. My brow furrowed but it did not give me pause. Picking up the delicate flute, a smile spread across my lips as I took the first sip.

"Don't move." A male voice sounded from behind me.

I froze, no fear swelled but apprehension sparked through every limb. Standing statuesque, warmth spread along my back. A presence taller than my own rested near, lingering with the promise of a touch. All I would have to do is relax, let my head tilt ever so slightly to feel the muscular chest I knew waited.

We remained like that for several minutes causing me to wonder if the other was as frightened to act as I was. Would I find rejection or lose myself in some stranger? Only the voice made me believe I knew who had arrived.

"Alexander." His name was a whisper from my lips.

Immediately I was spun around, my shoulders in the firm grip of a man whose gaze bore into my soul. My chest felt tight, heart hammering in search of an escape. When my lips parted, his eyes dropped to them only to succumb to the same need within. The moment his mouth met mine, I moaned.

The knowledge of how wrong this was somehow made it right. Who was I kidding, I had wanted this for so long I did not care. My body melted against his, the feel of his palm flat against my lower back sent heat up my spine. My own hands slipped up to tangle in his hair. Not breaking our kiss, he lifted me to set me down on the railing with his hips between my thighs.

A blush crawled up my chest to the tips of my ears. I gave myself over to the moment when he began to pull back. Sliding off the railing, my hands tightened at his back, my words a whisper between kisses.

"Don't stop. Please." I begged.

Without a word, he surrendered. In unison, we lowered ourselves to the floor. Laying side by side, I sat up and met his intense gaze. My right hand lifted to my left shoulder, the strap of my dress falling down my arm. Instantly he was leaning up to place the most tender kiss on the exposed skin.

That one small act made me gasp. Somehow his lingering lips conveyed everything neither of us were willing to discuss. A tear trailed down my cheek till his thumb brushed it away.

Silence was heavy between us, filled with all the words we dared not speak for fear of shattering this momentary escape.

When his lips parted, I rushed forward to seal them with my own. Desire long denied refused to be contained. Straddling his lap, my dress encircled my hips. Cool air pebbled my skin despite the warmth radiating from within.

My hands moved first, eager to feel him. Yanking his shirt off, the more of him I exposed the more lost I became. Nothing else existed except for us. Gone were all my worries about the future, my fear of ever being discovered for what we truly were.

When my fingers encircled his penis, my pulse kicked and I let a soft moan escape. Lifting myself up, there was no need for foreplay, I needed him as surely as I believed he needed me. He leaned his head down, my nipple hardening under the ministration of his wicked tongue. Pausing only long enough to stare deep into my soul as I welcomed him in, his head fell back while he drove his hips up.

My arms wrapped around his shoulders, his hands snaking up my back to grip me tightly. All I could do was steady myself as he drove into my body over and over again. It was awkward at first, our rhythm off as I tried to match his thrusts. Leaning back, our lips found each other, swallowing the grunts and gasps echoed between us.

One moment, I was straddling him, the next I was on my back beneath him. He slowed, one elbow on each side of my head, I could feel him sliding almost completely free of my body waiting a second then sliding slowly back in. Sweat beaded along his forehead, my own body becoming more sensitive the longer he maintained his torturous pace. His muscles bunched, veins pulsing with the control he exerted.

Coiled so much within, my hands grasped his ass to urge him to move. A devilish chuckle sounded against my lips, his tongue moved in time with mine, his hips pushing forward only to pause while we embraced. He pressed down, slowly rocking his hips. The pressure almost making every nerve in my body light up like the Fourth of July.

Then, he moved. Hips thrusting quickly, my core tightened around him as I welcomed the release. Crying out, I almost screamed with delight. Yet he did not relent. Purposeful thrusts kept my body on fire. Every inch becoming almost unbearably sensitive to his touch, his kisses, his cock. I could feel every inch of him sliding in and out of my body.

Another climax building, my nails dragged down his back just as his pace quickened. He left my lips to trail kisses down my chin to my neck then back up to that little spot just below my ear. As if there was a button there to press, another orgasm sprang to life throughout my body. Sweat coated my skin, the salty fluid mixing with his. Just as the waves began to subside, he jerked inside me. His cock pulsing with his own ending until he lay his forehead to mine.

We stayed that way for several minutes. Joined in silence. Small kisses shared without a word uttered between us. Something inside me fractured. A truth I did not want to admit to myself demanding to be acknowledged.

"I think I love you." I whispered.

"I know I love you, Beauty." Azrael replied.

Then he kissed me so slowly, so tenderly that I felt tears slip from each eye.

Waking up, I wiped at the tears covering my cheeks. A dream, it was just a silly dream. So why did my heart ache? Azrael was unpredictable, selfish, a man with no regard for the rules. There was always an attraction there, a curiosity. Always I chalked it up to a 'bad guy' fantasy.

At least in my dreams none of that mattered. In a dream, no one got hurt unless a demon or certain fae were involved. Letting a small laugh free, it felt good to remind myself of the facts.

Nothing wrong with any of it. Everyone dreams and dreams are safe to wonder what if. Just a dream and nothing more.

CHAPTER 31
~ ADEMIA ~

I had to smirk at all the vampires standing around. Each was a tense as priest in a brothel. There was no mistaking how each one despised my involvement with their little problem. Unfortunately for them, they had no choice but to admit they couldn't handle everything going on lately. Blood junkies were increasing in frequency in every territory. The more heavily populated an area, the worse it was. In more remote locations, mortals had begun to stay indoors when the sun disappeared into the horizon.

Vampires did enjoy making more superstitious folk start to wonder again about what lurked in the shadows. Even some of the vamps lost to their hunger taunted the mortals by leaving bloody bodies in the center of town with their throats ripped out. In the file, one instance of a gluttonous fanger resulted in bodies all lined up around a fountain. Heads were all removed to look up at their bodies that leaned over the edge. There were so many bodies, the water was almost a vampy temptation. I'm sure the picture didn't do it justice. Of course that was the last straw for the Elders. They demanded the extermination of all lost or even on the verge of being lost.

If all of us banded together we could make humans our slaves. Their salvation rested in the fact that no species as willing to rule alongside another. This is also why we can never let them know we exist. Humans would band together enough to wipe us out while we continued to try to fight on our own. Fucking pathetic but what can I say? I wouldn't want to work with any of these prickly bastards either.

"So, we all gonna just stand here and look pretty or you leeches going to show me the way?" I crossed my arms, my eyes meeting the one that appeared to be in charge.

"Follow me." She commanded after looking me over.

"Play nice and maybe I'll give you a taste." I ran a nail under her chin as I walked by.

She didn't react, just hastened her steps to lead the way up to the back patio of the estate. Waiting there was a table full of weapons, everything from a small crossbow, bolts, various handguns, and knives glistened in the lights on the wall. I picked up a beretta, lining up the site on the older looking bloodsucker on the other side of the offering. He shook his head mumbling something about impulsive demons.

"If you only knew, grandpa." I winked.

Setting the weapon down, I let my fingers trace the tips of the blades before turning to the assumed leader of the pack. She stood by, watching me, studying me for weaknesses no doubt. Perhaps even trying to guess what threat I was to them.

"For fuck's sake. I come in peace by the order of The Agora. You have nothing to worry about unless you're one of the leeches we are supposed to be hunting. So readjust your damn tampon and let's just get it over with. You don't have all night." I walked by on the way to the 6 black SUVs I saw behind all of them to the left.

"Hell's bells, can they be any more predictable?" I muttered as I slipped into the passenger seat of the first vehicle.

It didn't take long for them to join me. More exiting the house to follow as we began to leave.

"There are four sectors we are to clear tonight. Our last intel confirms there are approximately thirty to forty of the lost remaining. Given their unhinged state, they have proven difficult to dispatch." She kept her eyes on the road while I kept mine on her.

She was absolutely the one in charge of this lot. I had no way of knowing how old she was either but with how she held herself, I would guess she was pretty fucking old. Her accent was a muddled Spanish telling me she hasn't been home in a really long time.

Still, all of the information I surmised didn't mean shit. The most important thing was clear from the moment I stepped through the door. She was no match for me. None of those I had seen here were. Knowing they couldn't put up a real fight left me bored. My only hope now for some fun was to run into more than one of the fucking leeches gone wild at a time.

Pulling into an alley, I took note of the signs for the bars and restaurants occupying the building to our right. To our left was a tall brick wall separating this area from the expressway on the other side. The sound of the passing cars was the only noise the night provided to accompany the hunt. A smile grew along my lips at the thought of screams joining the symphony soon. On the other end, headlights flared to life signaling the other SUV was in position. They got out slowly, moving cautiously against the building while scanning the shadows for movement. I stood leaning against the hood, shaking my head at how ridiculous they looked. The security lights at every door made them visible while they attempted to be so discreet.

Pushing off, I pulled a curved blade from behind my back in each hand. Twirling them as I walked straight down the center whistling Mama Mia. The vamps paused, turning to watch me with obvious disdain. They seemed to forget the ones we were hunting had sharper senses than them due to being on the verge of complete insanity. If there were any here, they were already aware of us.

There were several little breaks in the dividing wall where overgrown brush came through to make its presence known. An easy place to hide until prey came near. As if commanded, a couple of women burst through a door on our right about 10 feet down. Their laughter as they leaned on each other for support confirmed why this was prime hunting ground. At seeing us, they fell silent and ran by wearily. If they only knew how much worse we all were than whatever they were imagining. Resuming my whistling, I changed the tune to Stone Temple Pilot's Wicked Garden. My demonic senses could feel the desire for violence. The source was drawing near yet the others appeared oblivious. Coming up to a door with a broken latch, I looked up at the sign. Old, weathered, the letters had faded so much I almost couldn't make them out.

"Come On Inn." I laughed, "Don't mind if I do."

Entering the building, the door creaked loudly. Pitch black filled the room with only a few shadows permitted entry by the boarded-up windows in the front. Here the smell of dried blood, violence, and sin permeated the air. My blades twirled in my hands in anticipation. I didn't try to sneak in or hide. What was the point? I wasn't some mook. They knew I was here, and I knew they were here. The only question was who was going to make the first move.

"I hear demon blood has a spicy taste to it." A gravelly voice spoke from within the darkness.

"I hear it tastes like a human barbecue." Another replied with a guttural laugh.

"Why don't you pussies come find out for yourselves?" I taunted; blades raised up ready for an attack.

I let fire erupt from my eyes, an apparent sign to them that the fight has begun. They did not disappoint though. From behind, one instantly landed on my back with fangs tearing into my left shoulder. Feeling my blood freely escape only spurred me on. Grabbing the vamp's head with both hands, the blades I held punctured the back of his neck as I yanked to flip him over my shoulder. He hit the ground hard, hissing up at me like some pissed off feline.

"Bad vampy." I pointed a finger down at him.

Dropping down, I jammed the curved blades on each side of his throat then slid them quickly to separate his head from his body. Blood sprayed up, droplets finding a home from my boots to my hair. I rose up even as his head rolled off toward the bar to the right. An angry cry drew my eyes five feet from the still twitching body. I leapt over, transforming part of the way as I landed. Shiny black horns, leathery skin, fiery eyes, and claws at the tip of each finger met the male who was waiting to strike.

Vaguely I became aware we were no longer alone. The doom squad had joined in which brought out all the vermin from their hiding places. All knew this was a fight or die situation. I didn't bother looking to see who was winning and who had fallen behind me. I relished instead that the one vamp had become three. A female and another male stood shoulder to shoulder with the first. All three moved in unison and each held their own dagger in their hands.

"Three against two." I raised my daggers, spinning them in my hands, "I like these odds."

"Bitch." The female spat out as they all lunged for me.

Going to take out the man to my left first, I jerked to my right when I felt a dagger pierce my side. Stabbing the man in the head, I let my blade remain to catch the middle leeches' knife in my hand. The cuts did very little, my hand igniting to melt the metal instantly. I shook my hand to remove the rest of the liquid before grabbing him by his throat. As the woman came forth to strike another blow, I sliced my remaining blade through her throat to leave her head hanging on by the slightest bit of skin. The man in my hold went wild, clawing at my hand and arm trying to get free.

Wagging my index finger of my free hand at him, I mouthed the word 'no' several times. As he kept fighting for freedom, I let the flames reignite in my hand to spread all along his body. Ash fell at my feet, and I wiped my hands together satisfactorily before bending to pick up my other blade. Moving quickly through the room, I stabbed another in the heart, removed another head, and burnt several more. When the room fell silent again, I was covered in blood, dirt, and ash.

Brushing myself off, the euphoria I felt at being free to kill kept a smile on my face. There was no waiting for the others, I just didn't care about any of them. I was ready to find more vamps to kill.

"Ademia." My name was called out only to be followed by a coughing fit.

Turning, I found the head bitch in charge leaning against a barstool. She was sweating, dirt clung to her face while a gash in her abdomen let blood dampen her shirt and pants. Tilting my head to the side, I shook my head as I leaned forward for her to continue.

"Help the survivors back to the vehicles." She grunted.

"Only if you say pretty please and ask nicely." I folded my arms.

She narrowed her gaze at me, if looks could kill, I would be the one turned to ash in an instant. What was with all these leeches and their inability to have a good time?

"Will you," she paused, taking a deep breath before continuing, "pretty please help the others?"

"Awe, I'd be happy to." I replied while moving to the closest vamp.

Grabbing his arm, I hoisted him up effortlessly till I was half carrying him out the door. Sixteen of us had started tonight's party. Five of us finished it. Once everyone was out, I set fire to the place before anyone could stop me. It was the best way to get rid of all the evidence if I do say so myself.

"Make sure you do not burn down the adjoining business-es." She said with a groan of pain.

"Please." She added when I raised a brow at her.

"Gladly, toots." I replied with an exaggerated bow.

She rolled her eyes but continued walking to the SUV. Remaining until the fire had done its job, we all headed back to the estate for them to treat their wounds and rest.

"Damn leeches." I muttered.

CHAPTER 32
~ SALAZAR ~

Fucking hell this felt right. Having her here with me, Purgatory was where we belonged. None could or would harm her while she was in this realm. Those that served as Reapers long ago saw me as their ruler. I didn't really care. However, being that I was just about the only thing that could end them into oblivion, they served me.

If it meant keeping her by my side, I would discard all of them. Seal off Purgatory for eternity and let the rest of the world do what it may. Of course, if she preferred, I would destroy all those on Earth. Doing so may be my end but for her, it would be done.

All beings have a weakness. Taking souls early uses a force flowing through us. It is that force which could destroy us if used too frequently or too greatly. Another way for the energy of all things to impose balance I suppose.

"A room is made up for you upstairs, down the hall on the left. If there is anything you need, simply let me know and it will be yours." I moved aside to let her take in her surroundings.

Not a fool, I was aware she was attempting to get an understanding of who I am by where I lived. The furnishings were meager. We had entered through the front door into a space filled with a couple of crème-colored tufted wooden chairs. A small oblong table sat between them with coasters and a small basket of lilies. The flowers I had added when she agreed to come here. On the walls were a few paintings, one of the clearing where Eve and I spent our time, only the cherry tree was standing tall in the center. Another one depicted the home where Eve and I had lived together and found happiness. The third was of Jenna, standing tall in boots, jeans, and a white fitted top with a black jacket.

The image was the day after she first awoke. She had stood out on the balcony of Marcus' home contemplating leaving for hours. I took the liberty of instead painting her standing in front of my home. Later I even updated the painting to include her white wings. Why hers were white continued to perplex me.

She stepped further into the room, her eyes lingering on the painting of the clearing. Some part of me hoped she recognized it while another feared she did and resented a memento of my time with Eve. The matter was truly confusing as she is Eve's energy, yet she is a new person as well. I love them both, but it is Jenna I need. She is fierce in a way Eve never was. Circumstances may have helped in making her this way, but she held it within regardless. It has been how she survived.

Ignoring the stairs to our right, she walked into the kitchen, open to both the first room and the next where the dining table sat. A large four burner stove was graced with her fingertips touch as she walked by. Opening the fridge, she took out a bag of chocolate covered cherries. Popping one into her mouth, Jenna passed me on the way up the stairs. How I longed to take her hand, but I knew better. Things needed to be on her terms. Jenna remained leery of me and my intentions.

Following behind her, our proximity did not help matters. The need to touch her, however small grew painful. Did she feel the same connection? Jenna is so guarded all the time that I cannot get a true read on her feelings.

"You're thinking too loud." Jenna's voice broke the silence.

"You are too closed off, so I am left to ponder what you think and what you feel. Unless you care to share." I replied.

"Ever thought of just asking, Jack? You're fucking Death and you can't ask a woman what she is thinking. Really?" She bit back.

"When it comes to anyone else, I do not care. With you, I have learned enough to give you control over most situations." I confided in her.

"Most?" She turned to face me as we stood between the bathroom door and the door to her room.

I glanced with a nod toward the bathroom, the meaning becoming obvious to her. She only rolled her eyes at me and entered her room. Still, I followed unwilling to leave her until she asked me to do so. I would end the world for this woman no matter the cost, yet she could crush me with a single sentence. Was this the purpose when the Gods first made her?

"When do we start?" Jenna looked over her shoulder at me.

"Tomorrow. Rest up tonight for you will need all the strength you possess." I informed her.

"Ok then. Goodnight, Jack." She took several steps away from me.

"Read this if you want to know more to both prepare and

perhaps, understand all which was done before." I set the journal I kept since first losing Eve on the foot of her bed and left.

She was here and tomorrow, she would learn the last of who she is.

CHAPTER 33
~ JENNA ~

The journal he left was surprising. As much as I attempted to keep myself detached from him, this log chipped away at my resolve as I had read it last night. At the same time, once more I was left wondering if he really saw me or only Eve. He loved her with all he is or was. How could there be room in his world for another? Even his home has memories of her and their life together.

Thumbing through the pages, I paused when my eyes landed on my own name. Preparing myself for being compared to his image of her, I sighed heavily before beginning to read.

~ Journal entry ~

She's awake. Jenna is awake. Soon she will remember her life as you, my dearest. She will remember the love we shared. Though, how do I confess to you how I have grown to love her for her differences as well. She has the same quick wit as you, but she is fierce in a way you never would be. Jenna has been eager to learn all she can about who she is and why she is. Spirits keep tabs on her for me and each regals me with her will to do more. Be more. Even before she was turned, she secretly despised the rules of society. To honor her father and mother she followed them though. The more she has learned of our world and herself, the more she embraces her independence. You are both kind to those in need. Yet Jenna does not stop with simply assisting them, she fights for them.

    I am in awe of her. Of whom she has become. The future holds endless possibilities for her because she chooses to keep going each and every day. Her compassion for all mortals confounds me but it is endearing at the same time. I love her, Eve. I fear perhaps even more than I loved you. Such a thing should not be possible. The ramifications of what this could mean for others is unsettling. She fits in a way I did not anticipate. For her, I would not just end the world, but I would save it if she simply asked.

A tear dripped onto the page; only then did I realize I was crying. The trust he desired was still not there but somehow, I felt a weight leave to know he saw me and not her. Salazar truly wanted me for who I am and not who I was. We would need to work on his eagerness to kill any and every one, but I could not say I blamed him for that.

One other problem remained too. Marcus. No matter how disgusted I am by his lack of empathy for humans, I caught myself missing him now and then. I needed my fucking head examined. Here I am, stuck between Death himself and a Demon Vampire who treats humans as cattle and my mind goes out to lunch while my heart and my cunt fight over which dick to desire. Of the two, Death was far more dangerous. His killing others would actually harm him allegedly, yet he would do it anyway.

A small knock on the door drew me away from reading more. On the other side was a young woman with Death standing behind her.

"Before you protest, please hear me out. She was to do today. Instead, I had her brought here alive for you to feed on for as long as you stay. She has agreed to this in exchange for living here and also helping around the house with tasks." He explained.

"I just weren't ready to die really. He tol' me whatya need and I'm ok withit and all. Other than when ya needin' me, I getta do what I like. Oh, an name's Rose, ma'am." Rose quickly added.

I could see the honesty in her words. She really was ok with spending her days as a walking buffet just to be able to live a while longer.

"Jenna." I held out my hand to shake hers.

Death's obvious relief made me suddenly think of Beauty and the Beast when he was trying to get her to like him. Another crack formed in the wall between us.

"Do ya need me now?" Rose interjected.

"No, thank you." I informed.

"Ok then." Rose waved as she turned to leave us.

"You have not eaten in a while. You do need your strength." Death stepped closer till he stood on the threshold of my room.

"I'm fine. I appreciate the thoughtfulness of finding someone willing who will not cause additional disturbances." I raised a brow at him.

He stepped further in causing me to take a couple steps back before my brain kicked in. Stopping, I remained in place until he was a breath away. Neither of us spoke, the words I read playing on repeat in my mind. When his hand lifted to cup my cheek, I automatically leaned into his warmth. Don't fall for this, Jenna. Be strong. Be strong. Be strong.

"I am going to kiss you now, My Missing Piece. I need to kiss you. If you allow it, I will worship you or if you wish, I will leave. Please allow me this one kindness first." Death's voice was deep, restraint tested in every word.

I nodded. It was all I found I could do. What harm could come from a kiss? How wrong I was. The moment our lips touched, the connection we share fought to lock into place. My pulse rocketed with the growing need for more. My lips parted in invitation, one that he accepted instantly. Our tongues dueled for control while our arms wrapped around the other's body.

Without conscious thought, I moved back in time with him to the bed. Turning him around, I pushed him back to fall onto the mattress. As he lay there looking up at me, I slid my shirt off over my head. Beneath the cotton fabric, I was bare, and the revelation was rewarded from him with a sharp intake of breath. My fingers slipping into my waistband, took no time dropping the pants I wore to the floor. Naked before him, I crawled on top, laying across him to savor his lips once more. His hands roamed freely over my body.

When he pulled away to remove his shirt, I stopped him with his head still covered to place a trail of kisses along his chest. Shredding the shirt, he had me on my back, his pants discarded in an instant. Raw heat exploded between us. Hands explored every inch exposed, while our mouths refused to leave the other's flesh. Nipping at his collarbone, he moaned while his hand raised to hold my head near his neck. No doubt about his offer, I bit down. His blood rushed into my mouth, the power within causing a shudder to reverberate through my every nerve. Holding me to him, he rolled us so I was back beneath him and with one quick thrust, seated himself fully within my core. He paused only a moment before giving himself over to his need.

Pulling back only to drive forward, my body tensed around him. I felt like I could feel him everywhere. He didn't slow his pace, hips thrusting harder and harder in an almost punishing rhythm. Licking the wound on his neck, we moved till he had me on all fours gripping the headboard for support. As soon as I was in position, he was pushing inside me. The walls of my core flexed around him, delighting in the stretching pleasure he demanded I take. His fingers dug into my hips, his lips occasionally lingering on my shoulder.

"Let go, Jenna. Surrender to what we are." He groaned.

The connection was almost a third person with us. Fear over what would happen had me keeping it at bay. Though the longer he fucked me, the lower the walls became. His hand reached underneath to twist my right nipple then massage the heavy mound. His fingers continued to alternate their attention from breast to nipple and back again. Suddenly his hand rose higher to catch me around my throat and making me stand on my knees while he used my body. His grip did not cut off my airflow but held firm so I could not move.

I lowered my hands to grip the back of his thighs while trying to meet him thrust for thrust. Moans accompanied the sounds of skin meeting skin as sweat began to bead. Then I lost, his other hand left my hip to press circles along my clit and send my first orgasm shooting through every limb. He refused to relent as I rode every last drop of the euphoria.

Pulled to the edge of the bed, once more he positioned me so I was on my back, this time with my ass almost off the bed. His eyes were a swirl of black and white when they met mine. Yet there was only a second to enjoy the enticing site. I saw him grip his cock at my entrance, grab my hips, and slide all the way inside coated by my release. What I had not expected were his wings to appear behind him as he did. The sight made my desire soar.

Wrapping my legs around his waist, I lifted myself still he held me by my ass while I rode him. Standing there, he held me, one hand helping me stay against him while the other fisted my hair to claim my mouth. Then it happened. I surrendered without thinking. White wings knocking things off the nightstand and with it, the connection locked in. We both held each other tight, a second release pulling a scream from my lips which he followed. His hips jerked, his cock pulsing inside me, a light surrounding us that was a mixture of white and black flames.

I was only faintly aware of them at first. Death held me in place, refusing to let go. I wasn't ready to either. Once we separated, we would have to go back to dealing with all the issues between us and the rest of the world.

"I..." He started but I silenced him with my hand.

"No. Just no. Don't ruin this. We are connected. Let that be enough." I urged.

He nodded, disappointment shining in his eyes. I wasn't

certain I felt the same or if I even could. One day, he may have to accept this for all there is and ever will be.

With that thought, I removed myself from him to then study the flames dancing around us. My fingers reached out to touch them to find they were not hot nor were they cold. To run my fingers through them reminded me of sitting in a warm bubble bath and running my fingers through the silky bubbles. The moment I moved away from Salazar, they subsided.

"What the fuck was that?" I asked.

"Hopefully me keeping my promise to show you what it's like when I intend to fuck you." He retorted with a smile.

"Ok, Jack. Seriously, what was with the damn light show?" I asked while finding clothes to wear.

"I don't know. I've never seen that before either." He confessed while seeming to study the ground where the flames had been.

"So, none of the other times you have been with someone, that happened?" I asked, finding it unsettling.

"The last person I was with was Eve." He admitted.

"Fucking hell." I shook my head.

"I don't think you are her replacement." He began.

"Enough. Let's just go train, ok? Then we can go ask Vanessa later if she has any information." I urged.

He nodded and led the way while dressing. Today was going to be a long day.

CHAPTER 34
~ SALAZAR ~

I led Jenna to the trees behind the house. Purgatory was not the barren wasteland many assumed it to be. At least, not since I took up residence here. Much of the landscape was filled with nature. Trees of every variety grew side by side. Streams flowed into rivers which let out into lakes. Modern conveniences were withheld from most as they needed to learn from their mistakes.

Darker souls were banished to an area where the land resembled a forest savaged by fire. The ground there remained hot, the trees never again recovering from the damage. Life in the forsaken wasteland was not one of ease by any means. Of course, others who did not really deserve such a fate were banished there too for disappointing or angering me.

Stopping beside a tall oak tree, I crossed my arms and waited for her to join me. She was taking in the surroundings with such scrutiny. When she looked me over, I could tell she was expecting me to strike. We would spar at some point, first we both needed to see how powerful she really is.

"I want you to let your wings out. Tap into your true essence without reservation. Then, when you are ready, send a targeted blow to the trunk of this tree." I patted the large trunk which was as wide as one of those ridiculously small cars.

"So, I'm a lumberjack now? Don't I get some flannel and a pair of suspenders?" She laughed.

"Just do it." I commanded.

She still hated being ordered around. Jenna's need for control was never ending. Fortunately, she knew this was necessary and she wasn't so spiteful that she would not try to learn. Rolling her shoulders a couple times, her wings emerged. They caught flecks of the sunlight which made them appear to almost glow.

Squaring herself off with the tree, her eyes swirled red. Black pooled into the crimson pool quickly followed by white. Slowly the white began to dominate, growing brighter till even her skin around her eyes started to shimmer. Throwing her left hand out, the trunk exploded, shattering into millions of pieces. Before the rest of the tree could fall, I pulled the energy from it, leaving it to become a twig.

Jenna panted, then turned to throw up. I wasn't surprised. She had just channeled a lot of energy through herself, far more than she ever had previously. The impressive part was how much she channeled and how quickly she was already recovering.

"What the fuck?" She stared at me.

"For a first attempt, you were very impressive. With regular training, you will be able to conjure even more with no ill effects. See, we are able to take the energy into us. It is how we can kill any and all beings. The downside is there is a limit or else we burn ourselves out. It is the only weakness we really have." I answered.

"There is something more, right?" Jenna rested her hand on a maple tree.

"If you give in to using the darker aspect, you drain all those nearby. The darkness is like a well that can never be filled. When judging a soul, the energy is fixated on the one. When you try to use it to kill, the energy pulls very quickly from the one but will eagerly jump to another as they cross into the afterlife. You have to learn how to turn it off effectively. Giving into how it feels having the energy fill you could be addictive. Go down that path and you will end up forfeiting your own existence." I explained.

"Were you always the only Death?" she immediately asked.

"No. There was a time when there were three of us. The others relished the power above all else. They found they couldn't get enough. One day, the scales tipped. Afterwards, when filling the void, some of our own life slipped away with it. Granted we have a lot and can regenerate but only if we maintain our own balance. The sources way to keep us inline I suppose. All this was long before most of creation so no one else knows of the others. They all assume I am and have always been the only Death." I confessed.

"I won't say anything." Jenna's voice held concern for me.

Turning back to the trees, I spread my hand towards them. Meeting her gaze, I knew she wasn't going to like what I was about to say.

"I want you to destroy all the trees in this area today. You will learn where your limits are. When you need to rest and how to focus the force of your attacks. Consider it a crash course." I instructed.

"Sure." She grumbled. "Only if you promise I get my official lumberjack shirt, suspenders, and honorary axe. I'll need a fitting name as well."

I sighed knowing part of her was serious about the name and maybe even the rest. With her, the sarcasm was sometimes a little hard to navigate. As I watched, she began knocking down some of the smaller trees one by one. This was going to make her ill but with the uncertainty of what was to come, I saw no other way.

Jenna needed to be prepared. I would protect her with all I am, but I fear her greatest threat is one I cannot anticipate. Herself.

CHAPTER 35
~ CARISSA ~

Jenna and Salazar have been gone for two weeks. Ademia has yet to return as well. Every day more reports come in, and every day Vanessa turns them all away. My frustration with her is growing. Things have gotten worse for the witches, spells have been going awry or not working at all. We now have a ward as well for vampires, werewolves, Lycan's, and other shifters who are half shifted and cannot shift back.

More and more, people are demanding to speak with the Host. They are scared and I cannot blame them. Fear has begun to turn into anger as well. Turning focus from the Host to Jenna and Salazar or Death as they know him. Many have requested the full story of why he brought Jenna into being and what she really is. Who she really is actually.

Mother has tried helping as much as possible, but we are both exhausted. Walking in, Vanessa appears once more to have slept soundly. Dressed in a light blue dress and barefoot, she runs her hands over the envelopes. Only this time, she screams.

"Get them back here. All of them. Get them back here now!" Vanessa begins crying.

Sending doors to each, it was Ademia who stepped through first. She was covered in blood and grinning from ear to ear. Moving to sit in one of the chairs, I made all the grime disappear from her body. Looking down at herself, she gave me a wink.

Salazar and Jenna came through shortly after. Both of them had wet hair with matching smiles. Seems things were developing between them while the world was slipping away.

"Someone was getting dirty in the shower." Ademia taunted.

"We don't have time for you two to get into a pissing match. Vanessa saw or sensed something and said you all needed to get back here. Now we can find out why. Vanessa, if you would please explain what is going on?" I motioned to her.

"There is a darkness, a very old darkness and it's coming for you. For all of you. Death, you weren't the only one to tip the scales, but they've been hiding. Now they are going to act. I saw Jenna and Ademia trapped in a stone room. Both shackled with a concealed presence." Vanessa looked as if she might cry as she spoke.

"Then I will go to see who it is. If they have chosen to act it will not be here. I'll leave The Agora so they can feel confident in coming after me alone. I know what you are going to say, Jenna. This is the smart play though and you know it." Salazar stated.

"Fuck you. You just want to play knight in raven wings. Got news for you. I'm not some damn damsel in distress. If I'm a princess, it's Princess Fucking Leia not Princess Peach. So, keep your balls on ice while I go get a few toys and we will set a trap together. Addy, come with me." Jenna didn't wait for anyone to reply.

Leaving the room, Ademia followed her while making an L on her forehead at Salazar.

"Tell her I'm sorry." Salazar stated.

"You know she's going to be very angry with you." I reminded him.

"I am aware, but I cannot stand by and let her be in danger if I can prevent it. After all, I am Death." He replied.

Even as he spoke the final word, he disappeared. I sat back in my chair preparing for their return and Jenna's livid response to his departure. Only minutes passed without a sound. Vanessa and I sat in silence, anxiety over what might happen building. Still, Jenna and Ademia did not return. A sinking feeling settled in my gut.

After twenty minutes passed, I could no longer ignore the feeling something was wrong. Opening the door to my office, I entered the room Jenna kept on-site only to find it empty. The weight in my stomach tripled at the realization of where they had gone.

"No." I whispered.

Going back through the door, I emerged in Jenna's apartment. It was also empty except there were signs things were not left peacefully. The large mirror was shattered. The coffee table was split in two and ash of at least five bodies littered the floor.

Quickly going through the door back to my office, a cold sweat broke out over my brow. No sooner had I returned than so did Death. Barreling into my office, he seemed to sense what had happened.

"Where is she? I suddenly can't sense her." He stood with wings unfurled and darkness swirling in his gaze.

"I don't know. She's gone." I replied.

"**W**hat the fuck, Lucifer? What are you doing? If this is about your precious demon. Get over it. You lost her." I yelled.

"This isn't about her. It's about you. You and the freak you keep turning to." He replied.

"What the hell is your problem? Tell me what this is about." I demanded.

He laughed, going over to where he had Ademia chained only to use his nail to cut along her abdomen. She didn't scream or even acknowledge the injury. Blood flowed freely from the gash to color the top of her pants.

"Do you know why you spared her? A fire demon. My own personal plaything." Lucifer taunted.

"It was an instinct, Lucifer." I confessed.

"Ah yes, your nature to protect innocent souls. She's a demon though. Didn't you find it odd?" He pushed.

"You're the fucking devil. You have thousands of demons. Why is my keeping her such a bee in your bonnet? You want to

come challenge me for her? Is that it?" I tried to free myself from my own chains.

"Absolutely not. I have actually felt freer not having her near." He sliced another nail across her chest.

"Then what, Lucifer? What is it you want?" I spoke through gritted teeth.

I wasn't a huge fan of any demon but to see her tortured was unjust. She wasn't even fighting back. How could she when she was bound the same way I was?

"Come on, Lucifer. We both know you don't have much time before others find their way down here. It will be war, Lucifer." I promised knowing the others were likely already looking for us.

"Lucifer?" He laughed louder, "You really think that some arch angel from millennia ago would go through all this? Are you really that delusional?"

"Then who the fuck are you?" I pulled at the bindings at my wrists and ankles relentlessly.

"I am hurt, Eve. Really, I am. Salazar wasn't the only one that felt your loss. It's his fault you died in the first place. Why can't you see that?! All of this is his fault!" His voice rose up to shake the walls around them.

Staring at him, a thought clicked into place, even as it formed, I rebelled against it. This wasn't possible. My eyes cut to the demons who had brought us here. Ademia's expression remained cold yet there was something in her stance that gave hope she too was just as surprised and perhaps pissed about this revelation.

"If you aren't Lucifer, where the Hell is he?" Ademia took a small step toward him as fire lit her gaze.

"Back off, bitch. He is nothing now." He turned her way, the demon flying back to slam against the wall she was chained to as he did.

"Adam." I stated with a calm I didn't feel.

Slow clapping filled the room. Lucifer. Adam turned with a wicked smile spreading across his lips.

"Ding. Ding. Ding. It's about time. You know after you died and your oh so precious Salazar left, some people in the village felt remorse. Then a couple started putting things together when they joined up to console one another. Maybe six months later, they all began to turn on me. You and your fucking monster ruined my life. All I wanted was for you to be mine. To bear my children. Cook for me. Clean for me. Marry me. Yet you had to go and love that thing."

"So, you became the devil? You really are a pathetic little man." I spat out.

"Don't say that!!" He screamed, his face less than an inch from mine.

I was startled but I refused to look away from his stare.

"I wanted to bring you back. To have you by my side and show everyone that it was his fault. Under the cover of night, I left to search out the witch everyone whispered about in the woods. She was of no help. I slit her throat when she told me I was mad. Afterwards I wandered here and there. Sought out anyone who said they could help." He recounted.

"I'm in this shit because you gave some guy fucking blue balls?" Ademia laughed from where she remained pinned against the wall.

"Adam," I spoke up when he stepped toward the demon, "what did you do?"

"I worked my way up. Learned rituals, languages, history, truth. There was a world all around us we never saw. The blinders fell away, and I could see Eve. Really see. I was able to cast a spell to stop me from aging. Next, I began communing with demons in search of Salazar. No one could find him. No one could find your energy either. One night, everything changed." He began to smile.

"Changed how, Adam?" I questioned.

"About a hundred years after your death, well before everyone started their new religious wars, Lucifer came to me. He isn't a bad guy really. However, he was over the whole '*devil*" rap. We ended up making a deal. I became Lucifer. Lucifer became no one or everyone. Not entirely sure how all that worked out for him. He checked in with me once or twice, but I haven't heard from him in, huh, I can't even recall exactly." Adam started laughing again, a smirk lingering that sent a chill down my spine.

"You really are a small-minded man. You're crazy. Completely out of your mind. I will never be yours. I don't give a damn if you were the most powerful being in the damn universe. I was never yours. Nothing you can do will ever change that." I yelled.

"You think this has been my only trick? How little you think of me is appalling. Shall I enlighten you on some of my other endeavors?" With a snap of his fingers, Marcus appeared in the center of the room.

"What the hell, Lucifer?" Marcus fell silent as his eyes found mine.

"Marcus. Explain now or so help me..." I felt the anger of betrayal well up from within.

"Jenna, it's not what you think." Marcus rushed out.

"Don't lie to the woman, Marcus. Tell her how you have been delivering souls to me in exchange for more power. How you have trapped and killed thousands of innocent souls for years now. All in the pursuit of becoming stronger than Death so you could win her back. It was the one thing we had in common. Of course, I lied. I was never going to let you have her." Adam taunted.

"All those people. The business you set up where you were selling off parts of people like some butchery. All because you were jealous? All you had to do was stop killing innocents. Stop harming those that did not deserve it. Then we could have had a chance. Now. Now I don't even want to look at you." I felt disgusted.

"Oh please. Once I heard what you were and your connection to Death, I knew I couldn't give up my business. I had already been helping Lucifer in exchange for keeping my demonic side free. My debt to him was one no one could erase." Marcus admitted.

"You will never change. I see that now. You're just like him. Only what you want matters. The how is of no consequence to you." I stated calmly.

At once, I was free. Marcus came near, his palm coming up to rest on my cheek. Drawing me near, he whispered before pressing his lips to mine.

"I will change for you." He said.

Kissing him slowly, the taste of blood trickled into my mouth. Marcus stepped back, eyes wide in shock. Falling onto his knees, before toppling to the side, his eyes never left mine. Tears fell silently down my cheeks. My hand dropping the dripping heart to the ground.

"If only you could have." I whispered.

Clapping brought me back to the here and now. Adam sat on a bench laughing while he clapped louder.

"Now that's what I call entertainment." He slung an arm around my shoulder.

Shrugging him off, I turned to face him. All around us was grey stone. No lights were visible, yet the whole space was lit well enough to see the circular room. One thing I noticed then was the lack of doors. No way for anyone from The Agora to enter here.

"It's just you and me now." He murmured.

"What am I? Just a piece of wall décor?" Ademia chimed in.

"Oh, but my precious fire. You are so much more than that. Here, I will let you both in on a little secret. To become Lucifer's replacement. I had to give up one pesky little thing, but I couldn't destroy it. So, with Lucifer's help, we created a powerful demon to hold it in. You, Ademia. See, you're actually Lucifer's daughter and inside, locked deep down is the reason Jenna wouldn't kill you. It's my humanity, my energy. It wasn't used to make you like with Jenna and her monster lover. You are just a pretty little box to hold it in." Adam's claw cut the bottom of her chin when he flicked his finger.

"Fight me. Let's end this once and for all." I stood my ground, ready for an attack.

"No, no, no. See, you are going to stay here until you come to your senses. This demon on the other hand has outlived her usefulness. I much preferred not having her around reminding me of Lucifer and what she holds. Thanks to Marcus, I have grown exponentially more powerful. So, I am sorry, Ademia, but this is where we part ways." Adam raised his hand as he spoke.

Ademia began to squirm until at last a scream ripped from her lungs. The sound reverberated off the walls, ceiling, and floor. I covered my ears and shut my eyes as the intensity increased. Moving was not an option, even breathing became ragged. Until everything fell silent. Slowly opening my eyes, I could not believe what I saw when I looked back toward her. Lucifer, the real Lucifer stood with Adam by the throat. His feet dangling about a couple feet off the ground.

"You broke our deal." Lucifer's deep voice sounded.

Without any hesitation, he sucked in a dark grey mist from Adam's body. Adam changed back to the man Eve once knew. Then he drained further until he was so frail a feather would likely knock him over. Part of me wanted to test that theory and often. He looked like someone who had been living without any real food or water for most of his life.

"He's still alive. We need to kill him." I shouted.

"No. My demon's will be dealing with him. Rest assured." Lucifer didn't look at me as he spoke, instead he released Ademia from the wall.

"Talk about an absentee father trying to make good." Ademia shot out.

"I would say we can talk further but the rules of The Agora remain in effect." Lucifer glanced my way.

"Ademia can stay to speak with you. Perhaps even get a little revenge for both of us on Adam. Though, I believe I will need her. There is still a lot to repair." I confessed.

"Just admit it, leech. You like me." Ademia teased.

"Surprisingly, Addy. You are growing on me." I laughed when she winced at the name.

"So how do I..." I didn't get to finish the question. One moment I was there, the next I was in the office of The Agora.

"You're back!" I exclaimed.

Salazar had Jenna in his arms before she could even acclimate to her surroundings. He lifted her chin, kissing her deeply as if he needed to reassure himself she was real.

"I am back. Adam is dead." Jenna stated then went into recounting all that had happened.

We all sat in silence. Taking in what she said and trying to make sense of it all. Salazar looked as if he wanted to kill someone, anyone, everyone. Jenna placed a hand on his though and the small act seemed to help subdue his murderous intentions.

"Then it's time." I announced, pulling the envelope from earlier out of my pocket.

"Ah, the special one. You going to tell us what this is all about? And do I get any time to rest?" Jenna asked.

"Don't worry, this shouldn't be too hard. Just depends on how you approach her." I explained.

"Her?" Salazar asked.

"Yes, it's time you go meet Jessica. She will help you reset the scales by bringing some of the clans together." I smiled at them.

"Which clans?" Carissa chimed in.

"Oh, I don't know. But it will be important." I replied as I watched them all sigh.

"Of course you don't. Carissa, mind whipping up some of the voodoo that you do so well?" Jenna laughed.

Without hesitation, Jenna was clean and armed. Salazar stood by her side ready to go.

"Oh, you shouldn't go, Death. Things won't go so well if you're there. Besides, you have to go check on some purple thing." I spoke up unable to see the purple thing clearly and wrinkling my nose.

"I think she means Jack Jr." Jenna laughed harder.

"I just almost lost you. Not ready to go through it again." Salazar pleaded.

"If you try to cage me, I'll run. So go play with your little friend and I'll be back soon." Jenna patted his chest.

Not even Death could control Jenna Devereaux. Stepping through the door, I caught a glimpse of a rundown bar on the other side before it closed.

CHAPTER 38
~JENNA~

"Whoever you are, I hope you're ready to get in some shit." I sighed, my eyes cutting up to the full moon above.

Walking into the place, it looked as expected from the outside. Wooden tables around a small dance floor where many were line dancing to the band on the smaller stage. A redhead waiting the tables in cowboy boots, jeans, and a top I could not read. Behind the bar was a blonde whose scent had me walking her way.

Vanessa didn't say the woman was of our world but I figured it was a good place to start. Giving the blonde a once over, she had her hair in a messy ponytail, no make-up, a black tank top with blue jeans. I assumed she wore cowboy boots as well. Sitting in the stool, she wiped the counter in front of me and looked my way without even the hint of a smile.

"What can I get ya?" she asked.

"I suppose blood is out of the question so how about a

whiskey on the rocks." I spoke evenly knowing she could still hear me over the music and stomping.

She grabbed a glass, setting it down quickly to fill. The longer I watched her, the more she appeared to anger.

"Have I done something? Spinach in my teeth?" I flashed my fangs.

"Whenever I run across others, seems things always end in a fight."

"I am not here to fight. Actually, I was sent to help. My name is Jenna." I explained.

"Don't care. And I don't need your help. Doing fine enough on my own." She replied before moving to the other side of the bar.

Giving her space, I sat there the entire night. Drinking and watching for what the possible threat could be. Maybe I wasn't here for her after all. Nothing appeared out of place and as far as I could tell, we were the only ones who were not human.

Closing down the bar, I waited in the shadows to follow her home. Turned out I didn't have to go far as she went behind the building to a small camper. Making myself comfortable up in a tree, I waited. Instinct told me she was the one. Now I just had to help her and convince her to come back to The Agora with me. I got the feeling neither task was going to be easy.

"How did I get so lucky? Fire Demon. Clueless Fate. Celestial. Death. Stubborn bitch to round things out. Of course, let's not forget the McKenzie boys." I scoffed.

Sitting in the silence, the recent events settled in. Marcus was dead. My fingers touched my lips as I shook myself to focus. I couldn't dwell on it now. With the scales swaying back and forth, I had to stay sharp. None of us knew what may come next.

A CHOICE FORGED BY FATE

~ To be continued...~

EXCERPTS FROM SALAZAR'S JOURNAL

She's gone. She's gone and all I wish to do is turn
this world to ash. It is only her smile in my memories
which halts my hand. Her laughter so filled with innocence which spares their lives. They do not deserve mercy
as she did not deserve to perish. For the first time, I
had purpose. I had joy. My life was no longer a meaningless chaotic rhythm of day upon day. They deserve to
wither for stealing her from me.

 I have kept her energy locked within her frozen
form, refusing to allow time to touch her. If I continue,
perhaps I will be granted leave to join her. I sleep now.
Exhaustion of the energies flowing through me requiring
such. She looks to slumber. Laying on the bed we once
shared so peacefully. I do not leave the chair beside her.
 I am Death. Why can I not then reverse the act?
Refuse its position to grant life? Every time I permit my

thoughts to wander they grow darker. Visions of those working the fields being blown away on the wind. The blacksmith's hammer falling from his grasp as his body disintegrates to nothing. Even the women cleaning their homes instead becoming that soot they attempt to sweep away. The children. All the children which would learn from those adults on being so naïve, so vile, going to sleep to never wake.

Then the blissful silence. Only the animals roaming the lands as it was very long ago. No arrogant men believing they owned all they desired. Living out my days with my memories and my grief. Yes, I wish to make them all pay. Every last one of them across this planet.

I never want to love another. To feel a loss as I do now. Betrayed by those she cared for. People she thought cared for her. Superstitious assholes. Kill them then keep them near to kill over and over.....

I woke this morning to find her gone. Truly gone now. Her body was taken from me. I have searched the town, those that attempted to refuse me were met with my wrath. Many were killed though the count is lost to me. My mind had one focus. Her. None had any lingering contact with her energy. Her body was not in any of the homes or shops. Adam was no where to be found yet somehow I do not believe this is his doing.

He is a coward. An obsessed, delusional man who will one day receive his due. Roaming as I searched, I cam to our clearing with the stump of the cherry tree mocking me. Stepping closer, a figure made of light took shape by the stump. His voice seemed to come from the wind all around me. He told me he had taken her and would be keeping her safe till the time was right. There was a prophecy which my involvement had interrupted. Now, the balance would be restored.

I yelled at him to return her, to keep his balance. Even as I did, my mind whirled. If there is a prophecy for her, then there is a way to bring her back to me. A way we can be together again. I left the field and have begun searching for someone who can see what is to come. I will find someone and make them tell me all I need to know. Then, I will bring my Missing Piece back to me. Once more I will be whole....

Months have passed. I refuse to fail you. Many have left me wanting. Many more have found their ends by my hands. Frauds who seek to earn favor attempt to lead me astray. Desperation drives me mad yet keeps me focused on securing your return. My Eve, my Missing Piece, where have you gone. One fortune teller hinted of another taking you and being permitted to do so in order to keep you from me. No matter the truth, they cannot keep you hidden forever. Time is a mortal tally, a way of organizing events. It is meaningless to me. Patience is not a virtue I maintain well but one I will endeavor to hold onto.

One day you will be back in my arms. Your body will be mine to worship, bringing you to cry out until your voice fails you. I will show you the depth of my feelings, of my need for you. My existence means nothing without you. Where I was once indifferent to the humans, now there is loathing. Only you can ease this ire.

My dearest Eve, we are all energy so I must believe in some way you sense my thoughts. Give me a sign, help me find you. I wonder if you are well. Are you aware of who holds you captive? Are you frightened? Are they hurting you? These thoughts will not leave me. They haunt my every waking moment and fill the dreams when exertion demands I rest. I am living my own Hell.

To be caught in this forsaken state only causes my desire for their end to rise. If I cannot have you returned to me, I will surrender to the command which repeats inside my head. How I long to make them each suffer as I am. Come back to me....

I have torn some pages from this journal. Pages you do not need to burden your eyes with reading. The time passed held the end for many. Even a few cities were wiped out overnight. Madness consumed me, I am ashamed to admit to you. If you were to know it all, you may never look upon me the same. Does not matter. I have found him. One who can foresee your prophecy. He is being brought to me tomorrow. A room is already prepared for him.

I will demand he write everything down in detail. After all, I did pay for locating him. A visit to the Fates who were not as accommodating at first. One had a soft heart for love though and convinced the others to assist me. She said she could see what I might do if left separate from you and felt the balance would be understanding. Her sisters warned they do not agree and believe my returning you forcefully will cause great harm.

For this, a price had to be paid. An agreement. A vow of silence. These three did not know how but they knew their end was near. One by one they would die to be reborn. The next three to arrive would also meet a destiny under a dark shadow they feared would be their death. Ridiculous as all knew, when speaking of the Fates' deaths it was always 'Two will die, One will live' as the balance needed one in existence.

Their request, keep the other two when they die. Stall the rebirth until the shadow lifts. I inquired on how I will know, which of course they cryptically stated simply that I will know. They do that shit just to be annoying I believe. I agreed to their demands. Only this journal, only you, will ever know of the debt. Just come back to me. Be mine. Fear me if you must. Love me regardless. I am yours to command....

I know where you are. Somehow you have been entrusted to a witch who resides in Hell. I have sent some to retrieve you. It has been so long many have forgotten of my existence. The anonymity aides in my efforts to bring you back to me. Soon. Soon you will be of this world once more. We will be together and any who wish to stand in our way will perish. In your absence, I have done something I never once tried before. I have expanded on my strength. Worked to hone my skills to an even more lethal combination. If the others continue to fail, do not fear. I will come for you. I will wage war on Hell itself to get to you if I must. One way or another, my Missing Piece, you will be mine.

AFTERWORD FROM THE AUTHOR

As an author, especially as an Indie Author, I am often asked how someone can help. To be honest, purchasing books legally is the best way to start but also reviews. Taking the time to leave some kind of review really helps the little-known authors get recognized.

If you choose to give your precious time to review my work, I thank you. If you don't, I am still thankful for you giving my book a chance. In either case, you are helping to make my dream come true and showing others that it is possible.